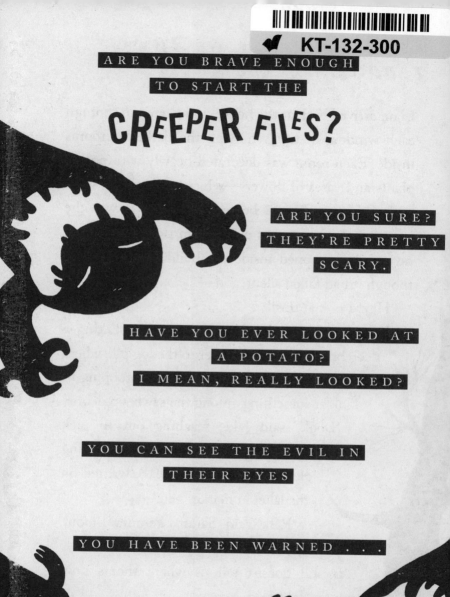

ARE YOU BRAVE ENOUGH

TO START THE

CREEPER FILES?

ARE YOU SURE?
THEY'RE PRETTY
SCARY.

HAVE YOU EVER LOOKED AT
A POTATO?
I MEAN, REALLY LOOKED?

YOU CAN SEE THE EVIL IN
THEIR EYES

YOU HAVE BEEN WARNED . . .

Liam arrived back at the house, and peered in through each window in turn, studying the darkened rooms inside. Each room was decorated heavily with potted plants and vases of flowers—which made sense, what with Professor Bloom being a botanist. It was the over-tidied interior that didn't seem right. As though no one had stepped inside the building in days. As though it had fallen silent, and—

'Hey! Look at this!'

Liam jumped as Jake's voice rang out. Taking a deep breath, he hurried over to the log pile where his friend, and now his sister, were stooping to look at something among the sawn-up debris.

'Look,' said Jake, reaching out to pick something up from the grass. 'It's a gardening glove, with the initials P.B. written on the label in marker pen.'

'P.B.,' said Sarah. 'Petunia Bloom. She must have dropped it.'

'It still doesn't tell us where she is now, though,' Jake said.

Sarah nodded. 'Liam was right, earlier . . .'

'Aha!' cried Liam. Then, 'Right about what?'

'Professor Bloom's car has gone,' continued Sarah. 'She might just have nipped to the shops.'

'Wearing only one of her gardening gloves?' Jake queried.

'Look, the other one's over here,' said Liam, spotting the missing glove poking out from behind the pile of logs. He stretched to retrieve it—

—then he screamed and fainted.

Jake and Sarah raced over to him.

'Liam! Liam!' yelled Jake, patting his friend's cheek. 'What happened?'

But Liam didn't reply. He was out cold.

'I don't underst—' said Jake, the words catching in his throat as he spotted the terrified expression on Sarah's face.

'I think he might have fainted because of that!' she breathed.

Jake followed her gaze to the glove Liam had plucked from the pile of logs. There was something inside which, now that it had been dropped to the ground again, had become dislodged enough for them to be able to identify.

It was a human hand.

OXFORD
UNIVERSITY PRESS

Great Clarendon Street, Oxford OX2 6DP
Oxford University Press is a department of the University of Oxford.
It furthers the University's objective of excellence in research, scholarship,
and education by publishing worldwide. Oxford is a registered trade mark
of Oxford University Press in the UK and in certain other countries

Copyright © Tommy Donbavand and Oxford University Press 2017
Illustrations © Lucie Ebrey 2017

The moral rights of the author have been asserted

Database right Oxford University Press (maker)

First published 2017

British Library Cataloguing in Publication Data

Data available

ISBN: 978-0-19-274728-0

1 3 5 7 9 10 8 6 4 2

Printed in Great Britain

Paper used in the production of this book is a natural,
recyclable product made from wood grown in sustainable forests.
The manufacturing process conforms to the environmental
regulations of the country of origin.

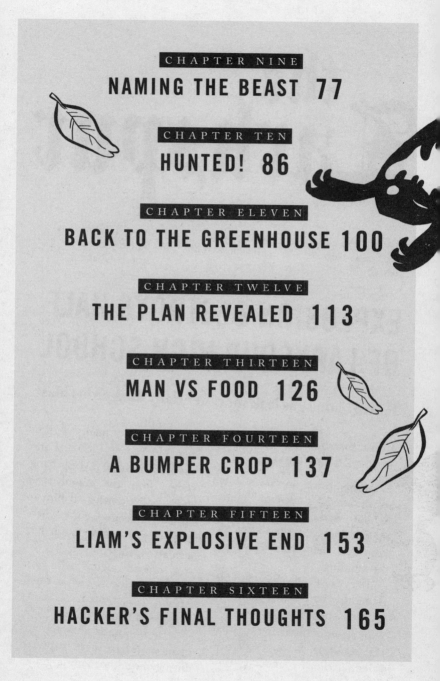

the Larkspur

EXPLOSION DESTROYS HALF OF LARKSPUR HIGH SCHOOL

Police blame gas leak for potentially dangerous blast

By our man in town,
HACKER MURPHY

Residents living in the streets surrounding Larkspur High School were evacuated from their homes yesterday, after an explosion demolished part of the building.

The cause of the blast is thought to be a broken gas main running beneath the school. Four crews of firefighters battled the resulting blaze, eventually bringing the fire under control hours later.

One local man, Arthur Spengler, 80, of Goose Lane, described hearing a big 'bang' coming from the school, after which, police evacuated him to Larkspur Leisure Centre where temporary accommodation had been arranged.

'I missed seeing who got through to The X Factor final,' Arthur commented. 'I don't suppose you know, do you?'

It is rumoured that the gas main may have been ruptured during one of the many upgrades

Chronicle

ALL THE NEWS YOU NEED THIS WEEK

ordered by the school's head teacher, Mr Irving Campion, although he denies the charge.

'It was nothing more than a devastating accident,' Mr Campion, 51, said at a press conference this morning.

'Thankfully, no one was injured or worse. So, it's time to put the incident behind us, and crack on with the work of getting pupils back to leading healthy, energetic lives. Now—no one leaves without taking an apple.'

However, one of the school's pupils—Jake Latchford, 13—had a different theory.

'You want to know what really happened?' he said. 'It was a monster. An inhuman, terrifying monster, who was more plant than person.'

Added Jake: 'And we haven't seen the last of him . . .'

CHAPTER ONE

HELLO FROM HACKER

Good morning. Or afternoon, if you're reading this then. Hopefully not 'good evening' though, because the last thing you want to be doing is reading this just before bedtime. Not if you want to sleep soundly, at least.

But I'm getting ahead of myself. Name's Hacker. I'm a reporter at *The Larkspur Chronicle*, which is arguably the best—and definitely the only—local weekly newspaper covering the Larkspur area.

Now, you might imagine that the life of a newspaper journalist is pretty glamorous. I bet you think it's all movie premieres, star interviews, and meeting sources in exciting locations.

You *might* think that, but you'd be wrong.

Every week, it's the same old rubbish—bonnie baby contests, tediously dull council meetings, school plays, people getting sponsored to sit in baths of beans, and notable members of the community retiring, dropping dead, or both. Sometimes even at the same time.

Occasionally, something interesting might happen somewhere in the area. A shop window might get broken. A fence might fall over. Someone might shout at someone else. Those were the stories I longed for. Those were the most exciting things that ever happened here in the sleepy town of Larkspur.

But that all changed last week.

It started with an explosion at the school. A gas leak, the police said, and while that was partly true, it wasn't the full story. Not by a long shot.

I know what really happened at the school that day. I know the terrifying series of events that led up to the explosion. And, more importantly, I know something else, too.

I know that this is just the beginning.

The police don't believe me, and my editor isn't interested in running the real story behind the exploding school. He thinks I'm just digging around, looking for trouble, but the truth of it is, trouble is probably digging around right now, looking for us.

I can't tell this story in the Chronicle yet, but I can tell it to you. Maybe it'll keep you safe. Maybe it'll keep you alive. Maybe—just maybe—the story that follows will help ensure you won't become a victim of the monster that stalks Larkspur.

A monster known only as the Creeper.

So, sit back. Get comfortable. Read over what I've been able to piece together of the story so far.

And should you hear a noise from the garden, or a soft tap-tap-tapping on your window, do not under any circumstances go out and investigate . . .

Your friend,
Hacker Murphy

CHAPTER TWO

BEWARE THE BROCCOLI

The giant head of broccoli rose up from the water, steam rising from every twisted stem and glistening crown. For a second, it paused, allowing any excess liquid to run away along its thick, green torso. Then it turned to face its prey: a boy, playing on his mobile phone, unaware of the threat posed by this vast victim-seeking vegetable.

Finally free of the water, the broccoli was lifted up into the air. It seemed to shiver—maybe from the change in temperature, but perhaps from the anticipation of the moment when it would appear before its unsuspecting quarry.

THUMP!

The bulging bulk of brassica landed squarely in

front of the boy. He recoiled, dropping his phone and opening his mouth to cry out . . .

'There's no way I'm eating that much broccoli, Mum!' exclaimed Jake Latchford, bending to pick up his phone. He gave his dog, Max, a quick tickle behind the ears while his hand was under the table.

'Then you won't be getting any dessert afterwards, will you?' replied Mum.

'But, look at it!' cried Jake. 'It's so big it's bending light around itself. I can't even see my chicken and potatoes any more. This thing should have its own moon!'

'You can moan all you want,' Mum said, placing the gravy boat in the centre of the table and taking her seat. 'But you're not leaving this room until you've eaten all your vegetables.'

'Vegetables?' beamed Dad, hurrying in and dropping into his own chair. 'Yum! The more the merrier for me, please!'

Jake's eyes lit up. 'You can have this big bit of—'

'Jake!' snapped Mum. 'Don't you dare. Eat your broccoli, then you can have some ice cream.'

'What flavour ice cream is it?'

'Cabbage,' said Dad with a grin. 'With sprout sprinkles.'

'You'd eat that, wouldn't you?' said Jake, shuddering.

Dad nodded. 'Too right!'

Despite his mood, Jake smiled. 'Weirdo!'

'Vegetable dodger!'

'No one's dodging anything,' warned Mum. 'And don't think you can get rid of your dinner by feeding it to Max under the table, either.'

Jake lifted his hand from his lap and dropped the stem of broccoli back onto his plate. 'How did you know?' he asked.

'She's a mother,' said Dad through a mouthful of roast potato. 'Trust me. They know. They know everything.'

Jake picked up his knife and fork. He held them, poised above the steaming pile of greenery. 'Oh well,' he said, suddenly not very hungry. 'Here goes.'

Twenty long, agonizing minutes later, Jake forced the final piece of broccoli into his mouth and chewed hard. Several hours seemed to pass until the lump was small enough to swallow.

'There!' he groaned, sliding his cutlery onto the empty plate. 'I finished it. But if I have some sort of allergic reaction and turn green in the middle of the night, it's all your fault.'

'Well, if that happens, we'll charge people a pound to come and see the amazing vegetable boy,' said Dad. 'Now, about that ice cream . . .'

'It's chocolate,' said Mum. 'But first—one of you can help me clear the plates away, and the other can take Max around the block.'

Both Jake and his dad grabbed their plates and stood. Mum shook her head and carried her own plate to the sink.

'We can't both clear the table,' said Jake.

'Let's toss for it,' said Dad. 'Heads or tails?'

'Tails!'

'I don't actually have a coin,' Dad confessed. 'Mum, heads or tails?'

'Heads,' said Mum.

Dad gave Jake a sympathetic pat on the shoulder. 'Oh, hard lines,' he said, trying not to laugh. 'Looks like you're walking off all that broccoli!'

With a groan, Jake grabbed Max's lead from the hook by the back door. 'It's just not my night, is it? Come on, boy . . .'

But Max wouldn't move. Instead he sat, glaring at the back door, and snarling.

'Max!' groaned Jake. 'I'm not in the mood for this. Come on!'

More snarls.

Sighing, Jake pulled on his coat and clipped Max's lead to his collar. He gave the lead a tug—but still Max stayed exactly where he was. 'What's wrong with him?

7

He's usually desperate to get outside.'

Dad shrugged as he reached for the now-empty gravy boat. 'Could be that new cat they've got at number 19. She's been winding him up all week—walking up and down on the fence like she owns the place.'

'He tries to get to her, but his legs are too little,' said Mum, whispering the words in case she hurt Max's feelings. 'Bless.'

'Well, cat or no cat—we're going out!' Jake reached out with his free hand to open the back door, then he pulled Max across the lino towards the exit with all his might.

'Don't forget to check my new petunias while you're out there,' said Mum. 'They were doing quite well the last time I looked.'

'Petunias,' said Jake. 'What colour are those ones again?'

'Pink,' said Mum. 'Well, pinkish-purple. Well, sort of purpley with a kind of lilac undertone to them.'

Jake blinked. 'Pink. Right. I'll take a look,' he said, practically dragging his dog out into the fresh air.

Outside, Max became even more upset. He began to bark madly and pull Jake along the garden towards the gate.

'I don't get it!' cried Jake. 'First you don't want to go

8

out at all, and now you can't wait for your walk. I wish you'd make your mind up!'

Max continued to bark, his ears lying flat against his head, and eyes darting back and forth.

'Suit yourself!' said Jake, looping the lead over the gatepost. 'Wait here for a minute while I check on Mum's flowers.'

Hurrying back up the garden, Jake kneeled on the cold grass and used the light from his mobile phone to check on his mum's budding flowers—but they weren't there. Instead, he found a handful of torn green leaves and the occasional pink or purple petal.

'Oh no,' said Jake to himself. 'Not again!'

Three times now in the past six weeks, someone had attacked gardens in this neighbourhood at night, tearing up flower beds, and generally ruining all the hard work put into their greenery by his mum and all their neighbours.

At first, blame was laid directly at the feet of young ruffians. The young ruffians quickly got together to issue a statement in which they denied any involvement in the garden-wrecking, and threatened to kick the heads in of anyone who said different. After that, everyone stopped pointing the finger their way.

Jake stood up and peered out into the darkness of the street, searching for—well, something that looked suspicious. The trouble was that everything looked suspicious in the fizzing yellow glow of the ancient street lamps. Even Dad's tool shed on the far side of the lawn had a distinct air of malice about it at night, and the worst thing that had ever happened in there was the time Dad's barrel of home brew ginger beer had exploded while he was testing the mixture. It took over a week of showers before the local cats would stop following him everywhere he went.

Glancing back at the house, Jake briefly considered heading back inside to tell his mum what had happened, but knew she wouldn't be happy if he didn't take Max out on his walk first. He fished a slightly crushed bag of salt and vinegar crisps out of his pocket and tore it open, eager to rid his taste buds of the lingering aftermath of broccoli. He tipped the bag up to his mouth, when—

CRASH!

The sound had come from further down the street. Could the flower-flattening fiend still be here? Still up to his wicked work? There was only one way to find out . . .

Easing the gate open, Jake slipped the crisp packet back into his pocket and allowed Max to lead him out into the street. The dog pulled and pulled, something he would normally be told off for, but on this occasion

Jake welcomed both Max's keen nose, and the fact that he could look quite big and scary under the right lights—and these were indeed the right lights.

So he let Max tug him along the road in the direction of the sound. Jake peered over walls and fences as they hurried along. Each one had been attacked by whoever—or whatever—was doing this. Plants had been torn up at the roots and scattered over lawns. Snapped stems and pulverized petals were all that remained of carefully tended flower beds. And, in one garden, the little gnome sitting at the edge of the pond had had his fishing rod snapped in half.

Was there no end to the evil currently stalking Larkspur?

Max picked up the pace. Jake could feel his heart pumping in his chest, and his palms were growing sweaty. Quite what he would do if he did stumble across a gang of motorbike-owning, tulip-despising ne'er-do-wells he didn't rightly know. Maybe it was time to arrange some backup.

Grabbing his mobile phone from his pocket, he hit speed-dial 2, clamped the phone to his ear, and tried to hear the ringing sound over the noise of Max's excited panting.

Eventually, the line connected with a CLICK!

'Liam,' Jake hissed. 'It's me.'

'Jake-a-roo!' cried Liam's tinny voice through the phone's speaker. 'I was expecting you to call . . .'

'You were?'

'Obviously! I mean—come on . . . You must have installed the new power pack for *Brick-Quest* by now! What do you think of it?'

Jake sighed. Of course. This evening was when the latest upgrade to their favourite computer game was due to be released. With the battle of the broccoli—and now a potential monster on the loose—he'd forgotten all about it.

'Well . . .'

'Tell me you've at least downloaded it!'

'Sorry, no . . .' said Jake. 'I'm out at the moment, walking Max.'

'Running Max by the sounds of it mate, you're out of breath.'

'Yeah,' gasped Jake. 'He's really going for it tonight.'

'So, if it's not to tell me that *Brick-Quest 2.8* is the best version of the game ever, why did you ring me?'

'It's the gardens again,' said Jake, 'they're—'

He stopped as Max's ears flattened back and he began to growl softly.

'What is it, boy?' hissed Jake, peering into the darkness.

And then he saw it. Standing in the next-to-last

garden of the street was a tall, extremely thin figure, silhouetted in the harsh yellow streetlight on the corner. The man—and it had to be a man—bent over and Jake could hear the unmistakable sound of flower stems breaking as the figure tore them from the ground.

Then slowly, deliberately, the man raised the handful of tattered blooms to his mouth—and he began to eat them. The figure chewed carefully as though he was savouring the flavours of a gourmet meal.

Then, Max barked. The man's head jerked in their direction, tendrils of half-eaten greenery dangling from between his teeth. Then he turned and started to walk towards them.

Pulling hard on Max's lead, Jake swung open the nearest garden gate and led his pet down onto a well-maintained lawn beyond. Like the other gardens, ruined flower beds said the thin man had been here as well, presumably making a meal of the owner's hard work. But he hadn't touched a thick hedge standing sentry near the front door of the house. Warning Max to stay silent, Jake pulled him behind the hedge.

The tall, thin man came closer—easing his way along the street while finishing off his fistful of flowers. Jake still couldn't make them out, but he could tell that the man's eyes were sweeping the shadows, searching for him. The creature was sniffing at the air too, as though he could discern the scent of living flesh from partially-devoured foliage.

All Jake had to do was stay absolutely silent, and he would be—

BEEP BEEP! BEEP BEEP!

14

Jake stared in horror as a text message lit up the screen of his phone. It was from Liam . . .

'You can design your own bricks!'

The figure spun to look straight at Jake. And this time he could see the figure's eyes.

They were glowing bright green.

CHAPTER THREE

THE HORRIFYING HALF-MAN

Max began to bark furiously, pulling at his lead, desperate to be free.

The figure glared down at the angry dog, seemingly unconcerned.

'Don't come any closer!' Jake warned. 'Max can be very ... bitey when he feels threatened.'

Bitey?! Jake thought to himself. *You're not exactly talking tough here. You might as well say he does big woof-woofs!*

Then the figure lifted a long leg, and started to climb over the garden wall.

Jake backed away even further. 'I mean it!' he said, trying to stop his voice from trembling. 'Stay back, or

I'll let him off the lead!'

But the shadowy figure didn't stay back. With its piercing eyes still fixed on Jake, it stepped completely over the wall and started to cross the lawn.

Then it reached out towards him with one of its arms, long twig-like fingers twisting and turning. The monster gurgled, almost as though it were laughing.

'OK!' cried Jake, swallowing his fear. 'You asked for it!'

His own fingers trembling, Jake unclipped the lead from Max's collar. 'Go on boy!' he hissed into his pet's ear. 'Do your worst!'

Both Jake and the dark figure watched as Max sped across the lawn, leapt over the wall, and then raced down the street in the direction of home.

There was a brief silence while both parties processed what had happened.

'Thanks a lot, pal!' Jake shouted after his rapidly-disappearing dog.

Then the tall, thin figure continued its journey across the lawn towards him.

'Right!' Jake said, his voice cracking. 'Slight change of plan. Come one step closer, and I'm calling the police!'

The figure came one step closer.

'Two steps closer, then!' cried Jake. 'Two steps, and

17

I'll dial 999!'

The figure took another step towards the terrified boy.

'Three steps!' shouted Jake. 'That's my absolute final offer! I'm really good at playing *Brick-Quest Lite* on here, so you won't believe how fast I can dial the number for the emergency services!'

One more step.

'Why won't you listen?' yelled Jake, his back pressed against the front door of the house behind him.

Suddenly, the security light above the door lit up, flooding the garden with the glare of a hundred white LED bulbs. *I must have triggered the sensor*, Jake thought to himself. He looked back at the creature who was still advancing.

Jake's thumb hammered down on the first 9 of the emergency number, but his hand was trembling so hard that he somehow dropped his phone.

'No!' he cried, eyes searching the grass at his feet. But he was still seeing swirls of colours from looking directly into the security light, and he couldn't find his mobile anywhere.

He rifled through his pockets, desperate to find another weapon with which to ward off this horrifying half-man.

All he had was a packet of salt and vinegar crisps.

It would have to do.

Plunging his hand down into the pack, he grasped a few fingerfuls of the salty snacks and hurled them directly at his advancing attacker's face.

To his amazement, the monster lurched back as they landed. Long, spindly fingers shot up to rub the crispy crumbs off whatever this thing had for skin, and the creature wailed in agony.

'Ha!' cried Jake, tossing more crisps at the bellowing beast. 'Thought you could attack me and get away with it, did you?'

The thing staggered back even further, hands raised to save itself from the onslaught of the deep-fried potato product.

Jake waited until he was sure the figure was too far away to suddenly reach out and grab him, then he, like Max before him, leapt over the garden wall and raced along the street for home.

'Glowing green eyes?' said Liam.

Jake nodded. 'They practically lit up the entire garden. Well, that and the security light. It's where I dropped my phone.'

Liam's sister, Sarah, paused to look over a wall at yet another scene of devastation. 'Which garden was it?'

'No idea,' said Jake with a shrug. 'Bit of a lawn, lots of torn up flowers . . .'

'That describes just about all of them.'

'There was quite a big hedge,' said Jake, recalling his hiding place. 'That should narrow it down a bit.'

'Why do we want to know which garden Jake was in?' asked Liam.

'I'd quite like my phone back,' Jake said.

'Oh,' said Liam. 'Yeah, fair point, well made.'

Sarah pulled a small plastic tub from her lunch bag and tore off the lid. 'Here,' she said to her brother. 'Want this?'

Liam gaped at a big wedge of chocolate and icing. 'Isn't that the cake you got at Eliza's birthday yesterday?'

'Yes,' said Sarah. 'But I need the tub.'

'Ace!' Liam beamed, grabbing the gateau and stuffing it into his mouth. 'Breakfast cake!'

Sarah tapped the empty container on a garden wall to get rid of the crumbs. 'I thought we could get a sample from the flowers this creature was eating,' she said. 'Then we could take it into the science lab and ask Professor Bloom to test it under a microscope.'

'Why would we ask Professor Bloom?' Liam wondered.

Sarah rolled her eyes. 'Because she's a botanist. She knows about plants.'

'Oh yeah,' said Liam, spraying cake crumbs everywhere. 'Another good point, well made.'

'Whoa, whoa . . .' said Jake, holding up a hand. 'We're not telling teachers or anyone else about what I saw! Especially not the deputy head!'

'Why not?' asked Sarah.

'Well, one—it makes me sound like a right head-case and, two—I ran away from the thing. In terror.'

'He's right,' said Liam, spraying yet more crumbs down his jumper. 'You don't go around school saying that you met a real life monster and then you ran away.'

'Well, I did,' Jake admitted. 'And you would have done, too.'

Liam shook his head. 'Not me. Anyway, I was right where I should have been, at home playing the new *Brick-Quest* upgrade. Isn't it brilliant?'

Jake shrugged. 'I've no idea!'

'What? You still haven't downloaded it?'

'I haven't had a chance!' cried Jake. 'Once I'd told my mum what had happened, she got me in the car and dragged me down to the police station to make a report.'

'What kind of report?'

'She reckoned I was just seconds away from being mugged.'

'By a tree?'

Jake stared back at his friend. 'You're not helping.'

'Sorry!' said Liam. 'But, you did tell her the twigs-for-fingers part, and the trailing roots, and the glowing green eyes, didn't you?'

'Of course!' said Jake. 'Well, a bit. By the time I got home I was starting to wonder whether I'd actually seen all that stuff, or if I was just suffering the side effects of a broccoli overdose.'

'You didn't describe this creature to the police at all?' asked Sarah.

'I tried,' said Jake. 'Well, my mum made me try. I got to the bit where I told them I'd managed to fight it off by throwing salt and vinegar crisps in its face and they stopped writing things down.'

'What?' said Liam. 'They didn't believe you?'

Jake shook his head. 'Mum took me back home and made me a cup of beetroot and chive tea. She said it was the best thing for someone in shock.'

'Ooh,' said Liam, wincing. 'More vegetables. Not a good result.'

'Tell me about it,' said Jake. 'So, no . . . we're not going to tell Professor Bloom what I saw last night.'

'OK,' said Sarah. 'We won't tell Professor Bloom . . .'

'Or anyone else . . .' Jake added.

Sarah nodded. 'Or anyone else. We'll go to the lab at break time and use one of the microscopes ourselves.'

'I can't do break time,' said Liam. 'Got a game of football against the year nines. Gonna be a belter, too.'

'Right, then,' said Sarah with a sigh. 'Jake and I will use one of the microscopes. If we can find any samples of the flowers the thing was eating.'

'Wait,' said Jake, stopping at a garden and peering over the wall. Like all the others in the street, its flower beds had been destroyed. 'This could be it. The house has got a security light, and there's a big hedge to hide behind.'

'And this is where you dropped your phone and shared your crisps with a monster?'

'No,' said Jake, 'this is where I hurled my crisps at an advancing nightmare that looked as though it wanted to suck my brain out through my ears! But yes, I dropped my phone.'

'Hang on,' said Liam, pulling out his own phone. 'We'll soon find it . . .' He quickly dialled a number, and then all three of them leaned in towards the garden and listened.

The theme tune from *Brick-Quest* began to play. It sounded muted and distant, as if it was far away.

'That's it!' cried Jake, straining his ears. 'My phone!'

He swung open the gate and darted across the lawn towards the thick hedge where he had been hiding the night before ...

... when the front door to the house swung open and an angry-looking man emerged. He had a bald head, and was wearing a baggy, off-white vest.

'This your phone?' he demanded.

Jake looked up from the ground to see what the man was holding.

'Yes,' he said with a grin. 'Did you find it out here this morning?'

'That's exactly what I did,' said the man. 'Along with what's left of my flower beds.'

'I know,' said Jake, surveying the damage. 'Terrible stuff.'

Suddenly, a horrible thought washed over him.

'Wait, you don't think it was *me* that did all this, do you?'

The man held up Jake's phone, which was still playing its jaunty ringtone. 'Well, this is evidence that you were here, isn't it?'

'Maybe not,' said Liam, wandering over to join Jake.

The man looked up at him. 'Eh?'

'You've got no proof that's Jake's phone at all!'

'Yes I have,' snarled the man. 'I was watching you

through the window. You dialled a number on your phone, and his phone started to ring. That's how it works.'

'Fair enough,' said Liam with a sigh. 'You've got us.'

'No, he hasn't!' spat Jake. 'OK, yes—that's my phone, but it doesn't mean I was the one who ripped up all your plants and flowers.'

'So, what *were* you doing in my garden last night?'

'He was throwing crisps at some kind of—' said Liam, quickly followed by 'OW!' as Jake kicked him in the shin. 'What did you do that for?'

'Sorry,' said Jake. 'I think I must have slept funny. Got a bit of a twitch in my leg today.'

He smiled pleasantly at the man in the vest. 'Yeah, I was here last night, walking my dog.'

Liam frowned. 'I thought Max came home by hims—OUCH!'

The man frowned. 'Do you normally walk your dog in other people's gardens?'

'Don't be daft!' chuckled Liam. 'He was in there hiding from—YEOW! Is there any chance you can make your leg twitch in a different direction, mate? I'm going to have a bruise there!'

The man fixed Jake with a stare. 'Go on. You were in my garden, hiding from . . .'

' . . . my dog,' said Jake, as matter-of-factly as he could. 'We were playing hide-and-seek.'

The man blinked. 'I'm sorry, did you just say you were in here playing hide-and-seek with your dog?'

'Yep!' said Jake.

'And, is your dog any good at playing hide-and-seek?' he asked.

'Nope!' said Jake. 'I found him almost straight away.'

'Does he play any other games, your dog?'

'Not really,' said Jake, shaking his head.

'No, just that,' said Sarah at the same time.

'Monopoly!' exclaimed Liam with a grin, which quickly faded when he caught his sister and best friend staring at him. 'Although he gets upset if you don't award him £10 for coming second in the beauty contest.'

'So, can I have my phone back, please?'

'Yeah, but I don't want to see any of you in my garden again!' The man handed the mobile back to its owner and disappeared back indoors.

Jake hit a key to silence the ringtone. 'Come on,' he said, walking away. 'We don't want to be late for school. We've got that new head teacher starting today.'

Liam followed, licking cake crumbs from his fingertips.

'Oh yeah,' said Sarah, 'I'd forgotten about him'. She

stooped to grab her school bag and, when she was certain no one was watching through the window, she scooped some of the partially chewed vegetation into her plastic tub.

Then she hurried after the boys.

'I wonder what he'll be like?'

LARKSPUR
POLICE

REPORT COMPILED BY: *Sgt Pamela Holgate*

DATE: *25th March*

TIME: *9.40p.m.*

Mrs Anna Latchford of 10 Duncan Street, Larkspur attended the station with her son Jake (13), claiming that he had been the victim of a personal attack while out walking the family dog, Max (age unknown).

At first Jake was reluctant to describe his attacker, causing me to wonder if he feared reprisals should an arrest eventually be made.

However, it soon became clear that the boy was making it up as he went along, describing a <u>seven-foot-tall plant</u> monster with green eyes that he had managed to escape from by <u>throwing crisps</u> (salt and vinegar).

REPORT COMPLETED: *10.02 P.M.*

Garden destroyer caught in the act?

Seven feet tall?

Fancy dress costume?

Crisps as Kryptonite!

CHAPTER FOUR

FIELD OF SHATTERED DREAMS

Finally, after a session of double French that seemed to last an eternity, the bell rang for break time.

Liam leapt out of his chair, stuffing his exercise book into his bag as he sprinted for the door. He'd been looking forward to this match against the year nines all weekend. Lee 'Curly' Harper had been getting too big for his boots lately—football or otherwise—and scoring a few goals past him before it was time for geography would be very satisfying indeed. If he could get in the game.

At the start of the term they had tried letting everyone who showed up join in, but it turned out that thirty-seven players on each team didn't improve the game of football at all. In fact, if anything, it rather ruined things. Especially for Billy Salter, who was driven away in an ambulance with at least three different players' shoe prints coming up as bruises on his freshly broken leg.

It was back to eleven-a-side after that.

Liam crashed through the doorway to the stairs, taking them four at a time and yelling at a clutch of tiny year sevens to get out of his way.

He hit daylight, and his heart sank. There were dozens of kids already lining up at the edge of the football pitch. There was no way he was going to get picked for the game now. It was bad enough that they only got fifteen minutes for break each morning— matches had to be seven minutes each way, with a minute spare to argue over whose turn it was to take the ball all the way back to the sports cupboard afterwards.

But, when he reached the edge of the playing field, Liam was amazed to see that no one was playing football at all. In fact, no one *could* play football. Because there was a huge red tractor busy ploughing the pitch up into long, even rows.

'What's going on?' he demanded.

'Dunno,' said Sickly Terry from year nine, spinning the ball in his hands. 'Looks like Woody's having some sort of breakdown.'

Liam peered closer at the tractor and saw that it was being driven by Professor Bloom's lab assistant, Woody Hemlock.

'I bet it all ends in a police chase,' said Sickly Terry.

'You what?'

'There's this programme I watch on telly,' Terry explained, '*Police, Camera, Edit That Bit Out* it's called. These things always end in a police chase down the motorway at 90 miles per hour.'

'But, Woody's driving a tractor ...'

'Alright, 20 miles per hour.'

'This is ridiculous!' barked Liam. 'I'm going to find out what's going on!'

Stepping out onto what had once been a beautiful football pitch, Liam felt his shoes sink into the soil of the freshly-furrowed field as he marched towards the tractor.

'You, boy!' cried a voice.

Liam turned, squinting against the sunlight to make out a tall man with a bald head and large, bristly moustache on the touchline. He was wearing a bright tracksuit and white trainers that had been cleaned to within an inch of their lives.

And he was jogging on the spot.

Liam had no idea who it was and, judging by the

looks of his fellow footballers, neither did they.

'Er . . . did you want something, mate?'

The man beamed. 'Yes!' he cried out. 'I'd like to give you the opportunity to run five laps around the school with me!'

Liam opened his mouth to reply, but the man was already sprinting away.

'Come on, laddie!' he shouted over his shoulder. 'The sooner you start, the sooner we're all fighting fit!'

As the rest of the gathered pupils began to giggle, Liam reluctantly gave chase.

Jake and Sarah peered around the door of the biology lab.

'Hello?' called Sarah. 'Professor Bloom?'

There was no reply.

'She must have nipped out,' said Sarah, leading the way into the lab.

'But she's always in here,' said Jake. 'I used to think she lived in here, until I saw her out in her garden one day, watering her plants. Her house is a mansion! Being a botanist must pay a lot.'

'She can't be that rich if she still has to work here,' said Sarah.

'Maybe she doesn't need the job,' suggested Jake. 'Maybe she just comes in each day because she likes the pupils?'

They both paused to have a chuckle at that idea.

'Do you reckon she was annoyed not to get the head teacher's job instead of this new bloke, whoever he is?' asked Jake.

'Maybe,' replied Sarah. 'Or maybe she doesn't want the responsibility.'

'She certainly doesn't need the money . . .' said Jake.

'Either way, we can't get her permission to use the microscopes if she's not here,' said Sarah, pulling the plastic tub from her backpack.

'If she's not here, then we don't need her permission,' Jake pointed out.

'Well, what about Woody? Is he around?'

Jake's eyes scanned the room again. Apart from himself and Sarah, it was still empty. 'Not unless he's mastered the power of invisibility.'

'Ha-ha,' Sarah mocked. 'I meant whether he was around here. You know, in the store cupboard, or in the bit out back . . .'

Grinning, Jake made for a doorway at the back of the lab. He grabbed the handle and gave it a hard tug.

The door groaned, but didn't move.

'Isn't it locked?' asked Sarah.

Jake shook his head. 'Not since those year eleven kids blew the lock off in a science lesson last year. It doesn't lock properly now. If you put a bit of effort in, you can just pull it open.'

Sarah smirked as her friend grew red in the face. 'So when are you going to start putting a bit of effort in?' she asked.

'I'm just warming up,' said Jake, blushing slightly. He stepped back, flexed his fingers, and tried heaving the door open again. 'Nnng,' he groaned, his muscles straining. 'Mmmf.'

'Just leave it,' said Sarah. 'If Woody's out there, he's clearly not going to be coming back in in a hurry.'

Jake ignored her. He didn't care who was out back now. Getting the door open had become a matter of pride.

'Almost . . . got it . . .' he grimaced.

'Your head's going to pop,' said Sarah. Then a sudden BANG made her jump. Fortunately, it wasn't the sound of Jake's head exploding, but was instead the sound of the door coming unstuck.

'See?' wheezed Jake, bending over with his hands on his thighs and gulping down deep breaths. 'Easy.'

Sarah looked past him at the little outside area at

the back of the classroom. Calling it a garden would be being generous. It was really just a small rectangle with the door at one end, a greenhouse at the other, and lots and lots of weird-looking plants in between.

Jake and Sarah wandered outside. 'Woody?' called Jake, although not too loud. 'Are you out here?'

The air in the garden tasted stale, and a tiny bit metallic. Jake was reminded of the day his dad had changed the batteries in an old TV remote control. They had leaked, and left dark stains all over the plastic inside.

That smell hung all around him, like unwanted relatives at Christmas.

Sarah brushed her fingers across a dinner-plate-sized rubbery leaf and gazed at the rest of the plants in wonder. Flowers bloomed. Vegetables sprouted. Branches and vines crept up the walls.

A tall hedge stood all around the garden, blocking the rest of the school grounds from view. Beyond the hedge, over on the right, was the football field. Normally, you could hear the thud of the ball being booted from one end of the field to the other, and the cheering of the kids running up and down the field after it, but today it was silent, apart from the distant chugging of some kind of engine. Weird.

On the left-hand side of the hedge was a little gate

which led out towards the car park.

And down at the bottom of the garden stood the greenhouse. Jake found himself drawn towards it. The old metal frame was rusting away, and the windows were almost opaque thanks to years of neglect.

Anyone could be in there.

Anyone. Or anything.

In fact, there seemed to be a shadow—unmoving, and just hinted at through the filthy glass. Almost the shape of a young tree, but one that was leaning backwards, not quite upright.

As though it was trying to pull itself up by its roots.

Jake reached out for the handle with trembling fingers, and—

A hand clamped down on his shoulder and Jake let out an involuntary squeal of terror.

'Any sign of him?' Sarah asked.

Jake slowly turned to face her. 'If he was here, I would probably have just scared him away by screaming like a four-year-old girl.'

'Oh, sorry,' Sarah said, trying to hide her smile. 'Did I make you jump?'

'Let's wait until my heart gets back under two billion beats per minute, and I'll let you know.'

Sarah hurried back inside the classroom and pulled the plastic tub from her rucksack. 'Well, if there's no one here to ask for permission, I guess we can just go ahead and use one of the microscopes.'

'Fair enough,' said Jake. 'Er . . . what for?'

Sarah rolled her eyes and opened the tub to show what was inside. 'I managed to grab a handful of those broken flower stems from that garden this morning.' She held the pieces of broken greenery up to the light. 'Look. You can see where that whatever-you-saw was chewing on the ends . . .'

'I told you!' said Jake.

Sarah switched on the nearest microscope. 'Pass me one of those glass slides,' she said, cutting a tiny bit of green stalk from the bunch and carefully centring it beneath the lens. 'If we can get a better look at the teeth marks, we may be able to identify what kind of creature it was, at the very—'

She stopped moving.

'What's the matter?' asked Jake quietly.

'I'm not sure,' replied Sarah. 'I've just got the strangest feeling that we're being watched.'

Cautiously, Jake leaned closer in to the tiny piece of chomped plant material on the microscope slide.

'Hello?'

'Not from there!' snapped Sarah.

'Oh!'

'Someone is behind us . . .'

39

The pair spun, expecting to discover someone standing behind them. But there wasn't anyone.

At least, no one *standing*.

Instead, a tall figure with a thick moustache and smooth scalp was down on the floor, doing press-ups.

'Good morning, children!' he said through deep breaths.

'Er . . . morning!' said Sarah, brightly. 'Are you looking for Professor Bloom? I'm afraid she's not here at the moment.'

'I already know that,' said the figure. 'She's at home today, unwell.'

'Really?' said Sarah. 'That's unusual.'

'And why is that?' asked the man.

'I've never known her to take any time off, for any reason.'

'Well, she has now,' the man assured her. 'She's at home. Under the weather.'

'Fair enough,' said Sarah, offering up a smile.

She didn't receive one in return. Instead, the man simply continued with his press-ups.

'Woody—er, I mean Mr Hemlock isn't here, either,' said Jake.

'I already know that as well,' said the figure. 'He's doing a job. For me.'

'Oh, I see,' said Jake. But he didn't, really.

40

'So, is there anything we can help you with?' asked Sarah, still smiling.

The figure jumped up and began to stretch vigorously from side to side. 'Yes,' he said. 'I'm trying to find out why, on a beautiful spring day such as today, when all the other pupils in school are outside enjoying the sunshine, I find two young people skulking in a dark science laboratory?'

Sarah swallowed hard. 'You're our new head teacher, aren't you?'

'Mr Irving Campion!' beamed the man, stretching out his hand for them to shake.

'We were just doing coursework,' Sarah lied. 'Jake was off sick during our last biology lesson, and I was helping him catch up.'

'That's very gallant of you, young lady,' said the new head. 'Giving up your precious break time in order to assist a fellow pupil. Well done!'

'Oh, I don't mind, really . . .'

'And I'm feeling much better now,' added Jake.

'I am delighted to hear it,' grinned the new head teacher. 'I think you'll find that everyone in school is going to start feeling a great deal better in the near future.'

BBBRRRIIIINNNNNGGGGGGG!

'Well, that's us!' said Sarah, reaching for her

41

rucksack. 'We'd better get a move on, or we'll be late for geography.'

The head switched from stretching from side to side, to bending down to touch his toes.

'Geography is cancelled, I'm afraid,' he said. 'As are all morning lessons.'

'No rush then,' said Jake. 'What are we doing instead?'

'It's time for assembly!' said Mr Campion. 'And we're going to hop, skip, and jump all the way there!'

Jake exchanged a glance with Sarah. 'We are?'

'We are indeed!'

Swinging back his foot, the new head caught one of his gleaming trainers in his hand behind his back— then he hopped off towards the classroom door.

'Keep up, you two!'

CHAPTER FIVE

THE NEW HEAD

Jake, Liam, and Sarah sat together in the assembly hall, raising their voices to be heard over the chatter of the other pupils around them.

'How was football?' Jake asked.

Liam shrugged. 'Well, the bad news is, we don't have a football field any more.'

'How do you mean?' Jake asked.

'It's a field,' said Liam.

'What's a field?' asked Sarah.

'The football field,' said Liam.

Sarah and Jake exchanged a glance. 'Well, yes,' said Sarah. 'I mean, the clue's in the name.'

'No, I mean it's not a *football* field any more. Just a field. You know, for planting stuff in.' Liam explained.

'The new head had Woody plough it all up with a tractor.'

'Oh. Right,' said Jake. 'So does that mean there's no more PE?'

'Oh, no. Twice as much, apparently,' said Liam. 'We're going to be using the big sports centre round the corner from now on.'

Sarah looked at her brother expectantly. 'Aren't you going to ask us how we got on?'

Liam frowned. 'At what?'

'In the lab,' said Sarah.

'What lab?'

'Professor Bloom's lab,' Sarah hissed. 'With the flowers.'

Liam blinked. 'What flowers?'

Sarah threw up her arms in frustration. 'Oh, why do I bother?' she cried, then she realized her voice was echoing around the now silent hall.

She looked up at the stage to find the head teacher standing behind the podium, staring at her. Sarah quietly cleared her throat. 'Um . . . carry on,' she said.

The head's stare lingered on her a moment, then he looked down and began to rifle through his speech notes.

The other teachers were all sitting uncomfortably on chairs behind their new leader. It was rare to see

44

any member of staff in assembly; pupil gatherings were usually seen as an excuse to hide in the staffroom with a cup of weak tea—but today, everyone was there.

Everyone except for Professor Bloom.

Sitting in her seat was a skinny young man with bright ginger hair and a stained lab coat. Woody Hemlock.

'Woody's looking happy with himself, don't you think?' Jake whispered.

'Only because he's chumming up to the new head by ploughing the football pitch,' muttered Liam.

'AHEM!'

A hush fell over the hall as the new head finally looked up from his paperwork. Slowly, he gripped the edges of the podium, swept his audience with a wide smile, and then cried out:

'Plums!'

The word echoed off the whitewashed walls.

'I'll be honest,' Jake whispered. 'I wasn't expecting that.'

'Apples. Celery. Cherries. Bananas. Cucumbers. Cabbages. Grapes.'

The room remained both confused and silent.

The head took a deep breath. 'Who can tell me what these things have in common?'

Liam raised his hand. 'They're all names rock stars

have given their newborn babies recently?'

'No,' said the head teacher. 'The answer is that they're all healthy—just like all of you are going to be.'

He paused dramatically. 'My name is Mr Campion, and I'm here to save your lives!'

'Two hours!' moaned Liam, rubbing at the base of his back. 'Two hours sitting perfectly still with my legs crossed on a hard, wooden floor. That wasn't an assembly. That was a new form of torture!'

The trio were heading along the corridor that led to the school canteen.

'We were there as well,' said Jake, 'and at least Mr Campion didn't pick you to go up on stage and demonstrate the correct way to do star jumps.'

Liam grinned. 'Yeah, you looked well daft!' he said. 'Luckily, everyone was too busy watching the school nurse help that year ten girl search her pockets for her inhaler to pay any attention to you.'

'He's a strange choice for new head teacher,' said Sarah.

'Strange?' scoffed Liam. 'He's bonkers! I never want to go through an assembly like that again.'

They pushed open the doors to the canteen and joined the queue for the counter. It was much shorter than usual.

'Did you get a new timetable?' Jake asked, pulling a sheet of paper from his blazer pocket.

'Yep,' said Sarah, finding hers. 'I think everyone did. What have you got after lunch?'

Jake ran his finger down the column for that day's lessons. 'Oh. Double maths.'

'Me too,' said Sarah.

'And me,' said Liam, reading his own timetable. 'But that can't be right. I'm not in the same set as you two swots.'

'Maybe you've been promoted for good behaviour,' Sarah suggested.

Liam shuddered. 'Then I demand a recount.'

He began to push his timetable away as they reached the counter. 'Two sausages and a large portion of chips, please.'

'Sorry,' said the dinner lady. 'No sausages.'

'What?' demanded Liam, looking up. 'How have they all gone so quickly?'

'They haven't gone,' the dinner lady explained. 'There are none.'

'But, it's Monday,' Liam continued. 'Monday is sausage day.'

47

'Not any more. New menu.'

Liam sighed. 'Alright, I'll just have the chips, then.'

'No chips.'

The colour drained from Liam's cheeks. 'N-no chips?' he stammered.

'Nope,' replied the dinner lady. 'New menu.'

'OK,' said Liam, taking a deep breath. 'How about bacon?'

'No.'

'Kebabs?'

'No.'

'Pizza?'

'No.'

'Curry?'

'Yes!'

'Really?'

'But, not today. And it's cauliflower korma.'

'What?' Liam spluttered. 'Why?'

'New menu.'

Jake stepped in. 'Do you have a copy of this new menu we could look at, please?'

With an exasperated sigh, the dinner lady disappeared into the kitchen and returned with a sheaf of papers. She flicked through them until she reached the right day, then handed it over.

Jake scanned the list. 'Oh dear . . .'

48

'Oh dear, what?' croaked Liam. 'Don't say "Oh dear". I don't want to hear "Oh dear" when it comes to my lunch.'

'I think you'd better sit down,' Jake suggested.

Liam's eyes grew wide. 'That bad?'

Sarah snatched the menu from Jake's hands. 'You two are like a pair of babies!' she snapped, reading down the list. Then: 'Oh dear . . .'

Liam gripped the edge of the counter. 'What could it possibly be?'

'OK,' said Sarah. 'Today we have a choice of . . . Vegan falafel wrap with rocket and kale, Boiled vegan burger with a slice of non-dairy cheese, Chicken-ish couscous on a bed of steamed lentils, and Non-fish fish-flavour fishcakes with spinach and sprout shavings.'

Liam slumped into a chair, looking as though he might burst into tears at any second. 'It's that new head!' said Liam with a snarl. 'This is all his fault!'

'The menu is certainly healthier than anything we've had before,' Sarah agreed.

'It's rabbit food!' Liam grunted. 'How am I supposed to concentrate in history if I haven't had a decent lunch?'

Jake frowned. 'You never concentrate in history,' he pointed out.

'Here . . .' said Sarah, plucking an old packet of cheese and onion crisps from the bottom of her rucksack and handing it over. 'There's no cake left, but I've got these . . .'

Liam reached out for the packet—only for it to be snatched out of his grasp. He jumped up. 'Hey—no one comes between me and my crisps!'

Mr Campion was standing there, peering intently at the list of ingredients on the back of the crisp packet. 'Is that so?'

'Well, except you sir, obviously,' Liam added quickly.

The room fell silent as everyone turned to watch.

Mr Campion flicked his gaze from the crisps to the trio and back again. 'Where did you get these?'

'I just had them in my bag,' said Sarah.

'You brought them from home?'

Sarah nodded. 'I must have.'

'They weren't bought anywhere here, in school?'

'No, sir.'

'Good, good . . .' Mr Campion closed his eyes for a second, then turned to address the canteen at large. 'New school rule . . .' he shouted. 'Absolutely no food whatsoever may be brought in from home from this point forward. Especially vile, disgusting items such as this!' He held the crisps high up in the air.

'What about the kids on packed lunches?' asked Liam.

'I'm arranging for these to be made on the premises,' said the head. 'As you were ...'

Then Mr Campion scurried towards the exit, arms waving about as though he were swimming through the air.

It took a moment for the sound of chatter to return to the canteen.

'He took my crisps!' groaned Liam.

'Seems as if that monster Jake saw isn't the only one who can't stand the things,' Sarah pointed out.

'That's right!' gasped Jake. 'That's too weird to be a coincidence. Why would they both hate crisps so much?'

'Don't ask me,' moaned Liam. 'I'm too hungry to think. You can't suddenly change an entire lunch menu and expect kids not to complain.'

'But who would they complain *to*?' asked Sarah. 'I don't fancy challenging Mr Campion anytime soon.'

'Yeah,' said Jake. 'He's a bit intense. And he'd probably make us do forward rolls around his office while we listed our complaints.'

'We could talk to Professor Bloom. If she were here.'

Sarah nodded. 'That's another thing. I can't decide

51

whether her being off school ill on the same day that a new head arrives is suspicious or not.'

'Everything about today is suspicious,' Jake said flatly. 'The new lunch menu, the two-hour assembly, Woody ploughing up the football pitch . . .'

'You're not wrong,' said Liam. 'I can't see how today can get any worse.'

BBBRRRRRIIIIINNNNGGGGGGGG!

'Double maths,' announced Sarah, slinging her rucksack over her shoulder.

'I stand corrected,' sighed Liam.

Together, they set off towards the maths corridor— only to find it sealed off with lengths of yellow and black tape when they arrived.

A sign stuck to the tape read: *Year eight maths pupils, report to the football pitch.*

Liam exchanged glances with his friends. 'Someone mentioned suspicious?'

'With a side order of bizarre,' added Sarah.

'Please don't use food references,' begged Liam, clutching at his rumbling stomach.

'Come on,' said Sarah. 'The sooner we get there, the sooner we find out what's going on.'

Reluctantly, Liam and Jake followed her to the pristinely-ploughed pitch—where they found both Mr Campion and Woody Hemlock waiting for them.

The head teacher looked on as the lab assistant handed out large, rough sacks.

'These are heavy!' said Sarah.

Jake peered inside his sack. 'That's because they're full of potatoes!'

'What?' Liam plunged a hand inside his sack and retrieved one of the small spuds from within. 'Do you think if I take a bite out of this and wish really, really hard it will taste like chips?'

'Good afternoon, everyone!' called Mr Campion. 'As you may have noticed, I've given you all a large bag of potatoes.'

'We'd spotted that, yeah,' said Jake, his legs almost buckling under the weight.

'As you know, Professor Bloom has a small allotment area out the back of her classroom, where she grows—among other things—all manner of fresh, wonderful vegetables,' Mr Campion announced. 'Do you know what I thought when I heard about it?' he asked, looking around the sea of faces, then pointing at Liam.

Liam hesitated. 'Uh . . . "what a complete waste of time"?' he guessed.

'On the contrary,' said Mr Campion. 'I thought, "what an excellent learning opportunity for us all!"'

He swept his arms out, gesturing to what had, until

very recently, been the football pitch. 'And so, we're embracing Professor Bloom's idea on a grander scale, learning about the wonders of nature, and growing some deliciously healthy vegetables for the canteen. Mr Hemlock has recommended that we begin with potatoes, because they're nice and easy to grow. Isn't that right, Mr Hemlock?'

'Yes, sir,' said Woody, 'and they are a wonderfully versatile vegetable. So many uses.'

'Mine look weird,' said a girl to his left. 'They've got all sprouts and stuff coming out.'

Woody took the potato from her and held it in front of him with both hands. It reminded Jake of the scene at the start of *The Lion King* when the monkey held the baby lion up for all the other animals to see.

'Those *weird sprouts,* as you call them, are the seeds of life itself!' Woody whispered. He glanced up and suddenly looked worried. 'Now, we must hurry, head teacher, for it will rain before the night arrives, and all these magnificent potatoes must be planted before that happens. They must not be allowed to get wet!'

'Oh, right,' said Mr Campion, taken slightly aback. 'I suppose we'd better get down to it, then.'

'Is it just me, or is Woody acting really weird?' Jake whispered.

'He always acts weird,' said Liam. 'He *is* weird.'

54

'Yeah, but not normally this weird,' Jake replied, but before he could say any more, Mr Campion loudly clapped his hands together, making everyone jump.

'Let our maths lesson commence!'

'I don't get it, sir,' said Jake. 'How are we supposed to do maths using potatoes?'

'I'm glad you asked!' said Mr Campion. 'It's simple really. You each stand at the end of a furrow and plant one of these seed potatoes into the ground, being careful to cover it fully with the soil. Then you say aloud: "one potato!" Take a small step forward, and repeat the process. Then you have "two potatoes", and so on.'

'Wait a minute!' said Liam. 'This isn't a maths lesson at all. I admit that, under any other circumstances I'd be thrilled about that, but you've just got us all planting potatoes instead.'

'And counting them as you go,' Mr Campion reminded him. 'That bit is maths.'

Grumbling, the pupils stood where Woody instructed until each furrow had a schoolchild and a sack of potatoes at the end of it. Then Mr Campion blew a whistle, and the planting began.

'If my back wasn't hurting from assembly, then it will be soon,' moaned Liam as he stooped to push his third potato into the ground. 'Three potatoes!'

'Something is very wrong here,' said Jake quietly to his friends. 'Four potatoes!' He dropped his voice again. 'And there's only one person we can visit who we can talk to about it . . .'

'Whoever it is, please tell me they own a pie shop,' said Liam. 'Four potatoes!'

'Six potatoes!' cried Sarah.

'Oi! Slow down, teacher's pet!' grunted Liam.

Sarah stuck out her tongue at him, then turned to Jake. 'Are you thinking of who I think you're thinking of?' she asked.

Jake nodded.

So did Liam. 'Yeah,' he said. 'I'm thinking of who you're both thinking of, too. Five potatoes! Alright, I'm not. Who are you two thinking of?'

Jake glanced up at Mr Campion and Woody to make sure that neither of them were within earshot.

'We're going to see Professor Bloom!'

Larkspur High School

LUNCH MENU FOR
Tuesday

As Implemented by Mr Irving Campion,
VSc. RBE. SC (level 2)
Head Teacher

∾ ✀

ENTRÉES
- Curried prune and fig soup with a dry roll
- Artichoke surprise

∾ ✀

MAIN MEALS
- Artificial egg salad doused with cucumber drizzle
- Celery burger and fried chipped parsnips
- Nuggets of prime seaweed coated in non-bread breadcrumbs

∾ ✀

DESSERTS
- Vegan milk ice-cream

(please note, no vegans were milked in the preparation of this product)

- A selection of greens

∾ ✀

DRINKS
- Water
- Cold water

CHAPTER SIX

LIAM GETS A HAND

Jake was right about Professor Bloom's house—it was practically a mansion. It stood behind ornate iron gates in its own grounds, protected by tall stone walls. Gardens spread out to the sides and around the back of the vast property, and a gravel driveway lined with lanterns led the way to a set of double doors.

Jake gripped the bars of the gates and peered through at the magnificent structure. 'See?' he said. 'Minted.'

'So, why are we here, exactly?' asked Liam.

'To talk to Professor Bloom,' said Sarah. 'I need her advice on the flower stalks Jake's monster was munching on.'

'And,' added Jake. 'We can find out what she knows

about the new head teacher and why Woody's acting the way he is.'

Sarah lifted the latch and swung open the right-hand gate. Liam rested a hand on her arm to stop her entering the property. 'What if she's not in?'

'Then I guess we won't be able to ask her anything.'

Liam nodded. 'It's just that her car's not here, is it? She's probably not here either. I think we should find another way to work out what's going on at school. Come on, let's get out of here . . .'

Jake smiled. 'Are you scared?'

'What?' scoffed Liam, puffing out his chest. 'Scared? Me?'

'Yeah, you.'

'No!'

'Really?'

'Alright, a bit,' admitted Liam, his chest deflating.

'Why?' asked Sarah. 'She's just a person like you or me. Well, me anyway.'

'No, she's not!' hissed Liam. 'She's a teacher!'

'And?'

'They're . . . different, aren't they?'

Jake blinked. 'I have literally no idea what you're talking about.'

'Yes, you do,' said Liam. 'They're, you know, *up there*—with police officers and dentists. You don't go out of your way to annoy them.'

Sarah snorted. 'I thought you went out of your way to annoy everyone.'

'Look,' said Jake. 'She's our biology teacher, and the deputy head at school. She's been off work sick, and we've just come round to give her our best wishes on our way home from school.'

'After first going home, getting changed, grabbing something to eat, and coming back,' Liam pointed out.

'Yes, after first having done all that stuff,' admitted Jake. 'Still, it's completely normal. She won't think we're weird.'

'She'll think Liam's weird,' Sarah said. 'But then, everyone does.'

Liam took a deep breath and nodded. 'OK, one— I'm not weird, everyone else is, and two—if we get told off, get eaten alive, or anything else happens, I'm blaming you two.'

'Fair enough,' Jake said.

The gravel crunched under their feet as they walked the length of the drive, lanterns lighting up as they passed each one.

'She's watching us . . .' warned Liam under his breath. 'I know it.'

Jake ignored his friend and rang the doorbell. There was no answer.

'There!' said Liam firmly. 'She's not in. Ah, well—we tried.'

Sarah grabbed the back of her brother's jumper as he turned to walk away. 'We're not leaving,' she said. 'At least not until we've had a good look around.'

'A look around?' demanded Liam. 'Have you two never watched a horror film? Big empty house, missing school teacher, some kind of monster tearing up flowers from people's gardens! There's no way that's not ending in tragedy!'

'Alright,' said Jake. 'You stay here while Sarah and I look around.'

'What? By myself?' croaked Liam. 'No chance. I mean, er . . . you might need me. You know, if things get dangerous.'

Sarah chuckled. 'The only danger around here is the danger that you might burst into tears at any moment. Come on, let's start around the back . . .'

The trio made their way along the side of the house, peering in windows as they went. The rooms inside were richly decorated, and there was nothing to suggest that anyone was at home, or that anything was amiss.

In the large garden behind the building, they found stacks of recently cut branches piled up against the fence, and an abandoned chainsaw.

'Ha!' said Liam, struggling to keep his voice from cracking. 'A chainsaw. Saw that one coming. Classic horror movie weapon, that.'

'Also a classic tool for cutting trees back,' Jake pointed out. 'Which the pile of logs would suggest is exactly what has been happening here.'

'It could still be a crime scene!' said Liam.

'No, it couldn't,' said Sarah. 'It can only be a crime scene if a crime has taken place and—the last time I checked—gardening wasn't a crime.'

'Fine, then let's look for clues,' said Liam.

'Clues to what?' asked Sarah.

Liam opened his mouth, hesitated, then closed it again. 'Just, you know, clues in general,' he said at last.

Jake shrugged. 'Maybe we can figure out where Professor Bloom is. Let's split up.'

'What?' Liam squeaked. 'Split up? Are you nuts? Did you hear *any* of my horror movie speech a minute ago?'

'Oh, shut up and go and check the house again,' Sarah said, giving her brother a shove.

As he stumbled off in the direction of the push, Sarah headed for a line of rose bushes which ran alongside the inner wall of the property. The green-eyed plant destroyer hadn't reached this part of Larkspur in his rampage, or, she had no doubt, these beautiful flowers would be stacked up with the dismembered tree branches, ready for the local tip.

Beyond the rose bushes, there was a small vegetable patch sitting silently in the last of the evening sun. Sarah made her way towards it.

Liam arrived back at the house, and peered in through each window in turn, studying the darkened rooms inside. Each room was decorated heavily with potted plants and vases of flowers—which made sense, what with Professor Bloom being a botanist. It was the over-tidied interior that didn't seem right. As though no one had stepped inside the building in days. As though it had fallen silent, and—

'Hey! Look at this!'

Liam jumped as Jake's voice rang out. Taking a deep breath, he hurried over to the log pile where his friend, and now his sister, were stooping to look at something among the sawn-up debris.

'Look,' said Jake, reaching out to pick something up from the grass. 'It's a gardening glove, with the initials P.B. written on the label in marker pen.'

'P.B.,' said Sarah. 'Petunia Bloom. She must have dropped it.'

'It still doesn't tell us where she is now, though,' Jake said.

Sarah nodded. 'Liam was right, earlier . . .'

'Aha!' cried Liam. Then, 'Right about what?'

'Professor Bloom's car has gone,' continued Sarah. 'She might just have nipped to the shops.'

'Wearing only one of her gardening gloves?' Jake queried.

'Look, the other one's over here,' said Liam, spotting the missing glove poking out from behind the pile of logs. He stretched to retrieve it—

—then he screamed and fainted.

Jake and Sarah raced over to him.

'Liam! Liam!' yelled Jake, patting his friend's cheek. 'What happened?'

But Liam didn't reply. He was out cold.

'I don't underst—' said Jake, the words catching in his throat as he spotted the terrified expression on Sarah's face.

'I think he might have fainted because of that!' she breathed.

Jake followed her gaze to the glove Liam had plucked from the pile of logs. There was something inside which, now that it had been dropped to the ground again, had become dislodged enough for them to be able to identify.

It was a human hand.

CHAPTER SEVEN

GETTING CLUED UP

Jake clamped his hand over his mouth, trying his hardest not to be sick. 'We have to get out of here, now!' he urged.

Sarah forced herself to look away from the severed hand. 'No, we stay and call the police,' she said. 'Plus, I don't know how easy it would be for us to carry Sleeping Beauty here with us if we ran.'

Right on cue, Liam opened his eyes and blinked hard. 'Is it still there?' he croaked.

Jake nodded.

Liam groaned and closed his eyes again. 'I hoped it might all be just a bad dream.'

Sarah pulled her phone from her bag, but Jake held out a hand to stop her from dialling. 'What if they think we did this?'

Liam sat up at that. 'He's right!' he cried. 'I can't go to prison. I've got too much to live for!'

Sarah sighed. 'Why would we turn up to see Professor Bloom, chop her into pieces—without getting a single drop of blood on our clothing—then hide everything except one hand and call the police on ourselves?'

Liam lay back down. 'She's got a point.'

'OK,' said Jake. 'Ring them . . .'

Ten minutes later, the call had been made. Sarah clicked off her phone and dropped it back into her bag. The sky above them had turned from blue to gold as an early spring sunset approached. A light rain began to fall as clouds gathered together overhead.

'So, what now?' Liam asked.

'We stay right here, and don't touch a thing,' replied Jake.

'You two are such wimps!' scolded Sarah, climbing to her feet.

Jake jumped up and helped Liam to do the same. 'What?'

'What are you talking about?'

'You both spend every waking minute playing that stupid computer game,' Sarah hissed. 'But when there's a real-life adventure playing out around you, you want

66

to sit and watch, or run away and hide.'

'Hey!' said Liam, raising his hand. 'I've been through a lot today already. I won't have anyone dissing *Brick-Quest* as well!'

Sarah folded her arms. 'What do you do in *Brick-Quest*? What's it all about?'

Jake and Liam looked at each other. They'd never really had to explain the details of their favourite game before.

'Well,' said Jake eventually. 'You have to mine bricks from the ground, and build castles and fortresses out of them.'

'Yeah,' said Liam, 'and then you can build up an army of warriors, and go out to attack other players' castles. Have a battle, nick their treasure.'

Jake nodded. 'It's two games in one, really. Dig and build—then attack and protect.'

'So, let's do that!' said Sarah. 'We can look around Professor Bloom's house—dig out and build up information for the police when they get here, and hand it over so they can protect us from whoever is attacking Larkspur.'

'I'm not sure that's exactly what the police wanted us to do when they told you to wait for them to arrive,' Jake pointed out.

'Maybe not, but what about you, Jake?' Sarah asked.

67

'What do *you* want to do?'

'Wet myself and run away crying,' Jake admitted. He sighed. 'Fine. You're right. We should take a look around.'

'Excellent!' cheered Sarah.

'But not in the house,' added Jake. 'We can't just go breaking in, we'll get arrested.'

'We'd only be breaking in a bit,' said Sarah, but Jake was having none of it.

'We'll look around the garden some more,' he said. 'Maybe something will turn up.'

'Yeah, like a foot,' Liam grumbled. 'Or a severed elbow.'

'I don't think you can sever an elbow,' said Jake.

'You can if you try hard enough,' said Liam. He puffed out his cheeks and looked around. 'So, what do we do?'

'We should split up again,' said Sarah.

'Or,' said Liam. 'We should all stick very closely together.'

'Oh, stop being such a chicken,' said Sarah.

'There's a hand lying over there on the grass!' Liam pointed out. 'A human hand, just sitting there all . . . stumpy. I think I'm well within my rights to be a teeny bit terrified, don't you, sis?'

Jake glanced at Sarah. 'He has a point. Safety in

numbers and all that.'

Sarah sighed. 'Fine. If it keeps you happy.' She started marching across the lawn. 'Come on, this way.'

Jake walked behind her, with Liam scurrying along at the back. His eyes darted left, right, up, down, searching for any sign of danger. It was early evening now, and the sun was starting to sink towards the horizon. Shadows of Professor Bloom's plants and trees crept across the grass, like fingers reaching towards the children.

Liam swallowed nervously. 'There's nothing here,' he said. 'We should probably just . . .'

His voice trailed off. His face turned pale. 'Wait,' he whispered. 'Wh—what's that?'

He raised a shaking finger and pointed to a shape at the bottom of the garden. The setting sun had turned it into a dark silhouette, but the outline looked worryingly like a man.

A man with a very large, very sharp-looking knife!

Sarah clamped a hand over her mouth. 'Oh, my goodness!' she squeaked. 'That's . . .'

'Yes?' whimpered Liam.

'That's . . .'

'*Yes*?!'

Sarah let her hand fall. 'A spiky bush,' she said.

A breeze rustled the outline, and Liam realized his

69

sister was right. 'Oh,' he said, smoothing down his jumper. 'Yes. I knew that.'

'Anyone see anything suspicious?' Jake asked. 'It all looks pretty normal to me.'

'Apart from the hand, obviously,' Liam pointed out.

'Yeah, apart from that.'

Sarah pointed down to a patch of muddy brown at the bottom of the garden. 'Did anyone check the vegetable patch?' she asked.

Liam and Jake both shook their heads.

'Nope.'

'Not me.'

Sarah set off towards the rectangle of furrowed soil. There were a couple of green stems sprouting up from below the ground, but the vegetable patch was otherwise completely bare.

'See anything?' asked Sarah, as they all snooped around.

'Oh no!' gasped Liam. 'Oh, please, no!'

'What?' Jake yelped. 'What is it?'

Liam bent down and plucked a small piece of plastic out of the ground. He held it up so the others could read what was written on it. 'She's growing *cabbages*.'

Sarah sighed. 'This is a waste of time,' she said. 'It doesn't look like there's anything here.'

'Yeah,' said Jake. 'Let's go back and wait for the police.'

They trudged, side-by-side, back across the lawn. In the distance, they could hear the faint screaming of police sirens getting steadily closer.

'Everyone ready?' Jake asked, stopping just inside the gate.

'For what?' asked Liam.

Jake's eyes narrowed. 'Um . . . for the police.'

'Oh, yeah!' said Liam. 'Forgot they were coming.'

Sarah was about to make a sarcastic comment when the ground beneath their feet rumbled. 'Whoa,' she said, looking down. 'What was that?'

'An earthquake?' Jake guessed.

'Um . . . I don't think earthquakes do *that*,' said Liam, pointing back down the garden in the direction of the vegetable patch.

Jake and Sarah followed his gaze. The soil looked as if it was churning, like there was something thrashing around deep beneath the surface.

'Is the ground . . . moving?' asked Jake, squinting to try to see better.

'I think so,' said Sarah. 'It's hard to tell from here.'

'Hand!' cried Liam. He bounced from foot to foot, pointing wildly at the vegetable patch. 'Look! Hand! Another one!'

The shadows made it hard to tell for sure, but even Sarah had to admit that the thing poking up out of the soil looked remarkably like a human hand, with fingers splayed outwards.

'You don't think Professor Bloom is buried under there, do you?' Liam gulped. 'The rest of her, I mean.'

'What do you think, Jake?' Sarah asked, but Jake wasn't looking at the hand. He was looking at the tall, spindly figure half-hidden in the trees behind it.

And he was sure the figure was looking back!

Suddenly, the three of them were surrounded by

screeching tyres, squealing sirens, and blinding flashes of blue light. They turned just as half a dozen police officers came leaping out of their cars.

Jake glanced back in the direction of the vegetable patch, but the figure had vanished. There was no sign of anything sticking out of the ground, either.

'Was it you lot who called us out?' demanded a surly-looking policeman with an even surlier-looking moustache. He looked at Jake, and his eyes immediately turned into suspicious slits. 'Here, you're that lad who came into the station yesterday, aren't you? Wasting our time.'

Jake forced a laugh. 'Haha. Yes. I mean, no. I mean . . . sort of,' he babbled.

'We're not wasting your time,' Sarah insisted. 'There really is a hand. We think something's happened to Professor Bloom.'

'To who?' asked the policeman.

'Our deputy head teacher,' Jake explained.

The policeman rocked back on his heels. He looked confused. 'What's she got to do with anything?'

'Um . . . she lives here,' said Sarah.

The policeman's eyebrows raised. 'Aha! Gotcha. Yes. That makes sense.'

He pushed open the gate. A woman in a white paper suit stepped through. 'Right, then,' she said, her

73

voice muffled by the matching paper mask she wore over her mouth. 'Lead the way.'

Jake, Sarah, and Liam stood by the fence, watching the policeman and the paper-suited woman down at the vegetable patch. They were deep in conversation, but every so often they'd glance up at the children, then down at the plastic bag the woman was holding.

'What do you reckon they're saying?' Sarah wondered.

'Looks like we're about to find out,' Jake said.

The policeman was trudging across the grass towards them, the plastic bag swinging from one hand. The other officers had spread out to look around the garden, and so Jake and his friends were on their own as the policeman huffed and puffed the last few strides.

'This it?' he asked, holding up the bag. The plastic was see-through, and all three children recoiled at the sight of the grimy garden glove.

'That's it,' said Jake. 'That's the glove with the hand inside.'

'Right,' said the policeman. 'Except it's not, is it?'

Jake and the others exchanged puzzled glances.

74

'It's a glove filled with wet leaves,' the policeman growled.

'What?' Liam spluttered. 'No, it isn't!'

'Yes,' said the officer, letting the bag open and the glove fall to the ground. It went *splat* on the grass, spraying mulchy leaves all over Jake's shoes. 'It is!'

Liam dropped to his knees and tipped the glove up. Clumps of soil and bits of root tumbled out, but there was no sign of so much as a fingernail, let alone a hand.

'But it was there,' Jake insisted.

'Now you listen to me, sunshine,' said the policeman, leaning down so his face filled Jake's entire field of vision. His moustache bristled as he spoke. 'If I catch you wasting police time once more, you're nicked!'

CHAPTER EIGHT

A WORD FROM HACKER

Hacker here again, but I won't keep you long.

Poor Jake. I can imagine how he must have felt when the police didn't believe his story for the second time in as many days. Following the explosion at the school (which we're coming to, I promise), I got a friend who works at the station to dig around in the police files, hoping to turn up something about the night Jake and his friends found the hand.

There wasn't even a report filed for the call-out, though, just a hand-written timesheet, with a single word scribbled on in red pen: Hoax.

It was no hoax, though. There had been a hand in that glove. As for where it went? Well, Jake would find out soon enough . . .

CHAPTER NINE

NAMING THE BEAST

'OK,' said Liam, tapping at the computer keyboard. 'All you have to do is grab the bricks from one wall and use the new *Duplicate* function to copy them to make the opposite wall . . .'

Jake leaned back on Liam's bed and rested his head against the wall. 'Gotcha.'

'Are you sure?' said Liam. 'Only it doesn't seem like you're very interested.'

'I am,' said Jake. 'Just tired. Go on . . .'

Liam hit the mouse button and scrolled down through the menu options. 'This bit is where the new upgrade gets really good,' he grinned. 'Once you've designed your own style for the bricks—wood, stone, ruby, whatever—you can port that all over your castle

77

in just a few clicks ...'

Max rested his head on Jake's leg, earning himself a scratch behind the ear.

'Sounds brilliant,' said Jake.

'Yeah, well you might want to tell your face that. You look bored stupid.' He gestured to the screen. 'What's wrong with you? This is *Brick-Quest*, Jake. *Brick-Quest*!'

Max began to snore softly.

Jake sighed. 'It's not the game. It's just . . . you know. Everything that's happened today. We found a body!'

'No, we found a bit of a body,' said Liam. 'A hand. And then it vanished again.' He shrugged. 'Maybe we were wrong. Maybe the glove was just full of leaves ...'

'But, you fainted when you saw it!'

'I think *faint* is a strong way to describe it,' said Liam. 'I was just a bit ... surprised.'

'Surprised to the point of unconsciousness,' said Jake, smiling for the first time that evening. 'I could have used that hand to pick your nose and you wouldn't have known anything about it.'

Liam laughed at the idea, then his face fell. 'You didn't, did you?'

The door opened and Sarah appeared. She flicked

a pair of Liam's pants off his bed with her foot, then sat down. 'Are you two seriously playing a game?' she scowled.

'Not exactly *seriously*,' said Liam. 'We're having a laugh.' He glanced across at Jake. 'Or, you know, we would be if he'd stop going on about severed hands and stuff like that.'

'Well, that's hardly surprising, is it?' said Sarah.

Liam frowned. 'Why?'

'Because we found a severed hand!' Sarah reminded him.

'Oh yeah,' said Liam. 'Fair point.'

'Did either of you tell the police about the vegetable patch going all . . . whatever it was doing?' Sarah asked the boys.

Liam shook his head. 'I was too busy freaking out thinking we might be arrested and questioned.'

'I didn't tell them either,' said Jake. 'They already seemed pretty annoyed at us. I figured it would only make things worse.'

Sarah nodded. 'That's why I didn't tell them, either.'

Jake leaned past Liam and took hold of the computer mouse. He slid the pointer over the X in the corner of the screen and closed *Brick-Quest*. The room fell silent as the upbeat theme music stopped playing.

'I saw him again,' Jake said. 'The green man. Thing.

79

Whatever he is. He—it—was in the garden, hiding in the trees.'

Sarah took a deep breath. 'I think . . . I think I might have seen him, too. Near the vegetable patch when it was churning up.'

'Well, that was him,' said Jake, quietly. 'That was the plant monster thing that chased me and Max the other night.'

'Then we need a better name for it,' said Sarah, grabbing the notepad and pen from Liam's bedside table. 'We can't just keep calling it the plant monster thing.'

'We can't?' said Liam.

'Not if we want to investigate him further,' said Sarah.

Liam's eyes widened. 'Well, we *definitely* don't want to do that, do we?' He glanced anxiously at the others. 'We don't, do we?'

Sarah nodded. 'We'll have to, if we want to find out what really happened to Professor Bloom.' She flicked to a blank page and clicked the pen. 'So, let's give him a name. What have you got?'

'Greenfinger,' suggested Liam.

'No,' said Jake. 'That sounds like something you'd go and see the doctor about. Or a really rubbish Bond villain.'

'OK,' said Sarah. 'How about Twiggy?'

'Wasn't there some fashion model from the 1960s with that name?' asked Liam.

'I dunno,' said Sarah. 'I just thought the thing's made of twigs and branches, so . . .'

'Branchy McBranchface, then!' giggled Liam.

'Be serious!'

'I am!'

'You're not! Jake, what do you reckon?'

Jake reached down to scratch Max behind the ear again. 'I don't know,' he said. 'I can see it every time I close my eyes, in that garden, getting closer and closer. Hands reaching out towards me, green pupils blinding me.'

Liam shuddered. 'Sounds creepy!'

'That's it!' exclaimed Sarah.

'Hands Reaching-out Guy?' frowned Liam.

Sarah scribbled on the paper then held it up for the others to read. 'The Creeper!'

Jake nodded slowly. 'That's it. It fits perfectly.' He took the notebook and stared at the name for a long time. 'The Creeper is attacking Larkspur,' he said. He tore off the page and ripped it in half down the middle. 'And it's up to us to stop him!'

The rest of the school week seemed to drag on and on. In addition to his changes to the menu, Mr Campion also made the wearing of trainers and sports shoes compulsory for all pupils. But only so he could also begin the day with a class-by-class five lap run around the potato field each morning.

Jake was panting and wheezing as he jogged along with his head down when Liam caught up with him during Friday's run. 'I can't take much more of this,' Liam said.

'We've only done one lap,' Jake pointed out.

'Not the running—well, yes the running. But the quiet, too. Things not happening.'

'What do you mean?'

'Where's the Creeper been all week?'

Jake grabbed his friend's arm. 'Not too loud,' he hissed. 'We don't want everyone to know about him. It could cause panic.'

Liam looked around. The rest of the class were trudging along, heads down. Some of the more red-faced ones at the back looked like they might even be crying.

'Mate,' said Liam. 'I don't think anyone's listening.'

'You never know,' said Jake. He glanced around. 'What's that old saying? "The walls have ears".'

'Yeah, but—'

'I know we're outside, and there aren't actually any walls around,' said Jake, quickly. 'It's just a figure of speech.'

They continued to run in silence as they entered their third lap.

'Is Sarah up in the library again today?' Jake asked.

Liam nodded. 'How she managed to convince Mr Campion that she should get out of this malarkey to research ancient exercise techniques in a bunch of old, dusty books is beyond me.'

'Well, don't knock it. It gives her the chance to read the botany books, too. If we're lucky, she'll find something we can use to stop the Creeper, should he ever show up again.'

'She wants us to meet up at lunchtime,' said Liam. 'She's going to let us know what she's found out so far . . .'

Jake felt a surge of hope. Sarah was great at digging around in books. If anyone could find out what the Creeper was—and how to stop him—it was her. With any luck, she'd have solved the mystery already!

'Nothing,' said Sarah.

Jake blinked. 'What, nothing at all?'

'Sorry. There's absolutely no reference to the Creeper—or anything that looks like him—in the school library books. I really thought he might have been seen around here before. That way we could learn how they managed to defeat him last time.'

'Who says he was defeated last time?' said Jake glumly.

'You are reading the right books, aren't you?' asked Liam. 'I mean, you're not just sitting around having a nice skim through a Harry Potter novel?'

Sarah rounded on her brother. 'I'll have you know that I'm working very hard up there—*and* keeping what I do a secret from Crazy Campion and his cronies.'

'Yeah, well try spending the week trudging through the mud, or sitting on the wooden floor in the assembly hall until your bum turns purple!'

'That's enough, you two,' said Jake. 'We're all doing our bit to make sure the Creeper can't hurt anyone.'

'Other than Professor Bloom,' said Liam. 'Who he's probably murdered.'

'Well . . . yeah,' said Jake. 'Apart from her, obviously.'

'I've been thinking . . .' Sarah began.

Liam hissed through his teeth. 'That's never a good sign.'

'We should come back and take a look at Professor Bloom's lab tomorrow.'

Liam's brow furrowed. 'What . . . on a Saturday? Have you gone mental?'

'There'll be no one else around,' said Sarah. 'It'll give us a chance to investigate properly.'

'But very much *won't* give me a chance to play *Brick-Quest*,' Liam pointed out.

Sarah turned on him. 'What's more important?' she demanded. 'Playing that silly game, or stopping a murderous monster from killing again?'

Liam considered this. 'Is it a trick question?' he asked.

'Sarah's right,' said Jake. 'We should come back tomorrow. I'll bring Max. I mean, he'll probably run away again, but maybe his nose will help us turn up some clues.' He looked across at the faces of his friends. 'So, are we agreed?'

'Yes,' said Sarah.

Liam groaned. 'I knew you were going to say that. Fine. Let's meet tomorrow. At school. At *the weekend*.' He sighed. 'What could possibly go wrong?'

CHAPTER TEN

HUNTED!

Next morning, Jake and Max arrived at the back of the school to find Liam and Sarah waiting for them. From her expression, it was clear that Sarah was raring to go. Liam, on the other hand, looked half-asleep.

'Did we have to meet so early?' Liam groaned.

'It's eleven thirty,' Jake pointed out.

'Exactly,' said Liam. 'On a Saturday. Who's awake at eleven thirty on a Saturday?'

'Everyone,' said Sarah. 'Literally everyone in the world.'

The back of the school was pretty featureless—lots of white-painted stone, and a few dozen windows. Jutting out from one part, though, was a tall rectangle of hedge. A metal gate at one end led through into

86

Professor Bloom's garden.

'Right then,' said Jake, looking the high gate up and down. 'Let's do this.'

Jake braced himself for the gate to creak ominously open when he pushed it, but it glided inwards without a sound. Max hesitated outside the garden, and Jake had to tug on his lead to get the dog to follow him inside.

'The back door's open,' Sarah whispered, nodding in the direction of the school. Sure enough, the door leading into Professor Bloom's lab stood slightly ajar.

'Maybe we left it open yesterday,' said Jake.

Sarah shrugged. 'Maybe,' she admitted. 'But let's go and look.'

'Yes, let's,' groaned Liam, trudging along through the garden behind them. 'It's not like there's a monster on the loose or anything.'

Inside the lab, everything seemed pretty much just as they'd left it. The slide Sarah had been looking at was still under the microscope, untouched. She had a quick glance at the piece of chewed-up flower again, but nothing seemed to have changed there, either.

'Were these here yesterday?' Jake asked, indicating two books that lay open on the professor's desk.

Sarah flipped the covers over to read them. '"*1001 Uses for a Potato*",' she read. 'And one about genetically engineered crops.' She shrugged again. 'I dunno. Maybe.'

'Uh . . . guys,' Liam muttered.

Sarah sighed. 'Yes, Liam, we know you're tired and don't want to be here, but just let us—'

Liam shook his head. 'Not that.' He pointed back out into the garden. 'That.'

Jake and Sarah joined Liam at the door. They both gasped at what they saw, and Max tucked himself in behind Jake's legs.

The greenhouse was glowing. That was the only way to describe it. An eerie green light was flashing and flickering inside, casting spooky shadows across the grimy glass.

Moving shadows.

'We should investigate,' Sarah whispered.

'Or run away,' Liam suggested.

'You're right,' said Jake.

Liam's face lit up. Jake pointed to Sarah. 'Sorry, I meant her.'

'Oh,' said Liam, deflating.

They made their way along the garden, Jake dragging Max along behind them. As they drew closer to the greenhouse, they could hear noises. Fizzing. Crackling. Groaning.

'Someone could be hurt,' Sarah whispered.

'Or about to be,' Liam squeaked. 'Namely us.'

The glass was so grimy they practically had to press their faces against it to see through. As soon as they did, Liam opened his mouth to scream. Sarah managed to clamp a hand across his face before he got the chance.

The inside of the greenhouse was a tangle of vines, leaves, and twisting branches. In the centre of it all was a chair—no, more like a throne. It had been formed from the tangled roots of a tree, which curved and snaked over the man sitting on it.

No, not the man. The thing.

Sitting on the throne, his eyes closed, was the Creeper.

At least, Jake thought it was. He was a little less plant-like than he remembered, and a tiny bit more human. Jake's eyes went wide. What if the Creeper was human, but could transform into monster form?

'Hurry,' the Creeper snarled. Jake and the others all tensed.

'Is he talking to us?' Liam gulped.

'No, look,' whispered Sarah.

There was another figure inside the greenhouse. It had a bulky, misshapen body, and its arms were two thick green roots. They wrapped around a large sack and carried it easily to the back of the throne.

89

'He looks like Mr Potato Head's evil twin,' Liam said.

The potato-man tipped up the sack, pouring dozens of plants, leaves, and other foliage into the back of the throne.

'I guess we know why he was ripping up all the flower beds in town,' Jake whispered.

As the walking spud continued emptying the sack into the throne, the Creeper seemed to grow larger and more plant-like. He spoke again, but this time Jake couldn't hear what he said.

The potato-man clearly heard, though. He nodded his stumpy head, then reached down and picked up a large, deadly-looking axe.

'I think it's time to reconsider that running away option,' Liam gulped.

'Shh,' hissed Sarah. They all watched as the potato-man raised the axe, swung it down, then . . .

CHOP! One of the Creeper's hands dropped to the floor.

'What is it with these people and chopping hands off?' Liam squeaked, turning almost as green as the plants around him.

'Look!' Jake said. To everyone's amazement, a new hand had already begun to sprout from the end of the Creeper's arm.

'Whoa,' said Sarah. 'Maybe that hand we found wasn't Professor Bloom's, after all,' she said. 'Maybe it was the Creeper's.'

Jake reached for his phone and tapped the camera app. He pressed the phone up to the glass. The police wanted evidence? He'd give it to them.

'Or maybe Professor Bloom *is* the Creeper,' he said, then he took a picture.

A bright white flash illuminated the inside of the greenhouse. The potato-man turned their way, raising the axe again.

'Uh-oh,' Jake muttered, as the Creeper flicked open his eyes.

'Run *now*?' Liam spluttered.

'Yes,' said Sarah. 'Run now!'

The gate was on the other side of the greenhouse. The Creeper had already started to detach himself from his chair, and the potato-man was lumbering towards the door. There was no way Jake and the others could reach the gate in time.

'Into the school,' he urged, pointing towards the lab door. Liam sprinted past him, screaming as he powered across the muddy vegetable patch. Sarah almost remarked that she'd never seen him so eager to go to school, but fear had made her throat tighten up.

Jake raced after his friends, just as the greenhouse door exploded outwards, showering the garden with shards of glass.

'He's coming!' Jake hollered, as they all hurried through the door and into the lab. Sarah tried to push the door closed, but the bottom was wedged tightly against the floor.

'Give me a hand!' she cried.

Liam grinned broadly and clapped, then remembered the monster outside and hurried to help his sister. All three of them shoved hard against the door. It groaned and shuddered as it inched slowly closed. Just before it did, Jake caught a glimpse of the Creeper stalking across the garden towards them.

'Crisps!' he said, when they managed to get the door shut. He slapped himself on the forehead. 'I should have brought crisps.'

'Bar of chocolate wouldn't have gone amiss, either,' said Liam.

'Not to eat! To fight the Creeper with,' Jake said. The door shook as something *thudded* against it from the other side. They all jumped back. 'The crisps hurt him, remember?' Jake whispered.

'We could get some from the canteen!' Liam said, then his shoulders slumped. 'Or we could have done, if Mr Campion hadn't got rid of them all.'

The door shook again. The children took another step backwards.

'Wait,' said Sarah. 'Crisps!'

'He already said that,' Liam told her. 'Weren't you listening?'

'No, I mean . . . it wasn't the crisps that hurt him,' Sarah realized. 'Salt and vinegar both kill plants! It was in one of the books I read!'

'Yes!' Liam cheered. He sagged again. 'But we don't have any.'

'Maybe not,' said Jake. 'But the canteen will.'

The door shuddered, and this time it opened a crack. The tip of a twisting tendril curved around the edge of the frame.

'Run again, you think?' Liam asked.

'Definitely,' whispered Jake.

'Yep, count me in!' Sarah agreed.

They skidded out into the corridor just as the back door flew open with a *crash*. They hurried towards the canteen, their racing footsteps echoing around the empty hallways.

'I knew nothing good could ever come from going

to school on Saturday,' Liam wheezed.

They weaved through half a dozen more twists and turns, until the double doors of the canteen stood dead ahead. From somewhere behind them, they could hear the steady *slap-slap-slap* of inhuman feet giving chase.

Liam clattered into the doors first, throwing them wide for the others to follow. The dining hall was in darkness, the only light coming from the narrow windows at the far end.

Jake's eyes scanned the tables. There were little tubs containing sachets of sauce, but there wasn't a single salt shaker to be seen.

'The salt,' he gasped. 'Where's the salt?'

Sarah's head whipped around, searching the canteen. 'They're gone! Mr Campion must have outlawed salt, too.'

Jake and Sarah's eyes met. 'Are you thinking what I'm thinking?' they both said together.

'Is it *we're going to die* by any chance?' Liam whimpered.

'Mr Campion must be the Creeper,' Jake said.

'That's why he's got rid of anything that can hurt him,' Sarah added.

The Creeper's footsteps echoed along the corridor right outside the dining hall. Liam gulped. 'Well, we'd better find something else, quick!'

Jake vaulted over the counter where the dinner ladies usually took the lunch money. A long-handled kitchen knife lay on a wooden chopping board further along the counter. Jake picked it up and gave it an experimental *swish*.

'This might do it,' he said, his voice trembling.

'Or these,' said Sarah, grabbing a pair of scissors from the top of the till.

Liam frantically searched around the worktop. 'Aha!' he cried, spotting a long handle sticking out of a plastic tub. He grabbed it and spun, twirling it like an expert swordsman. 'Let's see how the Creeper fares against this . . .' His face fell as he saw what he was holding. 'Flimsy plastic spatula,' he said, flatly.

There was no time to look for another weapon, though. The doors were thrown open, revealing a tall, plant-like figure in the doorway. The Creeper's eyes glowed green as he turned them towards the children.

'Wow, he's creepy,' Liam whispered. He blinked in surprise. 'Wait, I get it. *The Creeper*. Genius.'

The Creeper began to stalk towards them, his plant-like body *creaking* with every step. Jake's heart thudded in his chest like a drum. He clutched the knife tighter and tighter until his knuckles turned white.

'What d-do we do?' Sarah stammered. 'Should we rush him?'

'You two do that and I'll supervise from back here,' Liam suggested.

Jake looked the monster up and down. It seemed bigger and more terrifying than last time he'd seen it, from the top of its thorny, green head, to the tips of its twisted, twig toes.

Jake's heart skipped a beat as he spotted something on the floor in front of the Creeper. It was halfway between them and the monster. A tiny, white rectangle that was, Jake realized, their only hope.

There was nothing else for it. Jake launched himself forwards, barging past Sarah and Liam as he ran straight towards the Creeper. The monster began to speed up, vine-like tentacles extending from its back and whipping at the air.

'What are you doing?' Sarah cried, but Jake ignored her. He threw himself to the polished floor and slid across it, arms outstretched, grabbing for the little white rectangle. The cleaners must have missed it. Jake was so grateful, he'd happily kiss them all. Even the weird Russian one with the goatee beard and moustache.

OK, maybe not her, but definitely the others.

Jake let out a cry of triumph as his fingers found the discarded salt sachet. He jumped to his feet, tearing the packet open just as the Creeper made a grab for him. Jake slapped the open sachet against the side of the monster's face. Its skin—or moss, or whatever that furry green stuff was—began to hiss and sizzle.

The Creeper staggered backwards, tendrils thrashing as he growled in anger and pain. Jake shoved him hard, sending the monster stumbling into a stack of plastic chairs.

Sarah and Liam scurried over to join Jake, keeping their distance from the snarling Creeper. 'You totally *assaulted* him,' said Liam.

'Shut up, Liam!' Sarah snapped.

'Yeah, probably not the best time,' Liam admitted. 'Excellent joke, though, even if I do say so—'

'You still haven't shut up!' Sarah pointed out.

'Oh. Yeah. Shutting up now,' Liam said.

'Let's get out of here,' Jake panted, and they all hurried towards the door.

Halfway there, Jake realized something was missing, and had been for a long time.

No, not something. *Someone.*

'Max!' he yelped. 'Where's Max?'

98

He spun on the spot, searching the dining hall, but he knew it was useless. He knew exactly where Max was.

'I left him back at the lab,' he said, his face turning pale. 'We have to go back and get him!'

CHAPTER ELEVEN

BACK TO THE GREENHOUSE

Jake and the others clattered back into the lab and pushed the door closed behind them. 'Max?' Jake called, his eyes darting around the room. 'Max, are you in here?'

'He must be outside,' Sarah said.

'Unless he's been eaten,' said Liam. He caught his sister's look and shot Jake a reassuring smile. 'Um, which he definitely won't have been!'

'You two go and find him,' Sarah urged. 'I'll keep looking in here. There must be something that'll help us stop the Creeper!'

Jake nodded. 'OK. Be careful,' he said.

'If you die, I'm getting your room,' added Liam. He

100

ran after Jake, stopped, ran back, gave his sister a brief hug, then darted after his friend again, shouting, 'But try not to!' over his shoulder as he ran.

Sarah glanced nervously at the door. She couldn't hear the Creeper approaching yet, but she was sure he'd be on his way. She puffed out her cheeks and looked around the cluttered lab. 'Come on, Sarah, think,' she whispered. 'There has to be something you can use.'

Jake dashed out into the garden, keeping low as he searched for Max. He bent double, checking under the hedge and bushes, but there was no sign of the little dog anywhere.

'Where is he?' Jake whispered. 'Where could he have gone?'

'Definitely not eaten,' Liam said, forcing a smile that was far too broad. 'No way. Definitely not.'

WOOF!

Jake spun in the direction of the sound. The greenhouse! Max was in the greenhouse!

Unfortunately, the dog wasn't alone.

Through the hole where the door should have been, Jake could see his dog yapping and growling at the misshapen brown figure looming above him.

'It's that potato guy!' Liam whispered. 'He's not looking. Let's mash him!'

'Yeah, but—'

'Let's turn him into chips!'

'OK, but—'

'Let's knock the stuffing out of him!' Liam said. 'I mean, I know that one doesn't really make sense, but I couldn't think of any more potato things to say.'

'Liam, look!' Jake said. He pointed to the potato-man, who still hadn't moved a starchy muscle. 'He's frozen to the spot like a statue.'

'Oh,' said Liam. 'Yeah. So he is.'

'By the way,' Jake began, 'you could have said, *let's give him a roasting.*'

'Argh!' Liam groaned, throwing his hands in the air. 'That would've been brilliant! Why didn't I think of that?'

'Come on, let's grab Max and get out of here,' Jake said.

Back in the lab, Sarah looked up from Professor Bloom's desk. She held her breath, her heart suddenly crashing. Was that . . . ? Had it been . . . ?

Yes! Footsteps outside in the corridor. Close, and getting steadily closer.

Sarah darted to the door and saw Jake and Liam in the greenhouse. At first, she thought they were being attacked by the potato-man, but quickly realized he was standing completely still.

'Jake! Liam!' she hissed. They both turned at the

sound of their names. Sarah jabbed a thumb back in the direction of the door. 'Someone's coming. Hide!'

The boys both nodded. Sarah threw herself under Professor Bloom's desk and squeezed into the narrow space. She pulled her knees to her chest and tucked her face in behind them, trying to quieten the panicky sounds of her breathing.

Out in the greenhouse, Liam and Jake both made a grab for Max. The little dog was still barking madly at the potato-man, though, and he scampered out of reach when the boys tried to catch him.

'Shh, Max. Shut up!' Jake whispered.

'Sit!' Liam commanded.

Max ran in a circle, still barking.

'Stay!' Liam ordered.

Max ran back and forth across the floor. Still barking.

'Run around and bark like a maniac!' Liam instructed.

Max ran about and barked like a maniac.

Liam tutted. 'Bum. I thought he was just doing the opposite of everything I said.'

Jake made another dive for the dog. His fingers brushed against Max's collar, but then Jake's foot snagged on a trailing root.

'Waargh!' he wailed, as he stumbled, thrown

103

off balance.

Max stopped barking as both he and Liam watched Jake go flailing across the greenhouse, headed straight for the glass. Before he went crashing through the windows, though, he collided with the tree-stump throne the Creeper had been sitting on, and fell into it.

Jake sat there for a moment, getting his breath back. 'That was close,' he wheezed. 'I thought I was going head first through the glass for a second.'

'Yeah. That could've been nasty,' said Liam.

Jake looked down as the throne suddenly squirmed beneath him. Long, vine-like tendrils snaked up his arms and legs, pinning him in place.

'Though probably not as nasty as that,' Liam muttered.

Max shot into the corner and lay there, shivering with fear. Jake tried to pull his arms free, but the vines had them pinned. The tendrils tightened, and Jake cried out as they almost cut right into his flesh. They continued to snake up his arms and across his shoulders. Jake shuddered as they crept and crawled through his hair and knotted together at the top of his head.

'Wh-what's happening?' he yelped.

Liam winced. 'Um . . . I don't know. But if I had to guess, I'd say "nothing good".'

104

The throne began to vibrate. The air around it seemed to fizz and crackle, like it had suddenly become charged with energy. Jake strained against the bonds.

'Don't just stand there!' he pleaded. 'Help me!'

'Oh, yeah. Of course. Sorry,' said Liam. He looked the chair up and down. Jake's arms and legs were almost completely covered by greenery now. 'How?' Liam asked.

'I don't know!' Jake yelped. 'Find an off switch or something.'

'It's a tree,' Liam pointed out. 'They don't generally have off switches.'

'They don't generally tie people up, either!' cried Jake.

'Fair point, well made,' Liam admitted. He stepped closer to the throne and searched for anything that looked like a button. After a few seconds, he spotted a big round knot in the bark, which was slightly raised above the rest of the wood.

'I found it!' he cheered. He pressed the knot. Nothing happened. 'Oh, no, false alarm.' He chuckled. 'It was just a knobbly bit of the tree!'

'Why are you laughing?' Jake hissed.

Liam's face fell. 'Oh, yeah. Sorry.' He was about to go back to searching for a switch when he spotted something in Jake's ear. He leaned in for a closer look, then chewed his lip. 'Um . . .'

'What?' said Jake. He tried to turn his head to see what his friend was looking at, but the tangle of vines had him held tight.

'Nothing,' said Liam, but the shake in his voice betrayed him.

'What is it, Liam?' Jake demanded.

'It's just . . . It's just . . . ' Liam swallowed, then tried again. 'It's just that your ear's sprouting leaves.'

'What?!'

'It's probably nothing,' Liam said. 'I'm sure it's completely normal and nothing to worry about.'

'Of course it's not completely normal!' Jake yelped. He struggled harder against the vines. They creaked and groaned, but didn't budge. 'It's the chair! The chair's turning me into a plant monster like the Creeper!'

Liam nodded slowly. 'I mean, yes, that is certainly a possibility,' he said. He reached into Jake's ear and yanked the leaf out.

'Argh! That hurt!' Jake said. 'Stop mucking around and help me!'

'How?'

'The axe! The potato-guy had an axe. Get that!' Jake said.

Liam's eyes widened. 'I am *not* cutting your ear off. You know what I'm like around blood.'

'Not my ear, cut the vines!' Jake barked.

'Oh. Yeah. That makes much more sense,' Liam muttered. He spun, searching for the axe, then let out a high-pitched shriek when he spotted it. It was clutched in the hands of a figure who stood in the broken doorway, half-hidden by the frozen potato-guy.

'Woody?' said Liam.

'Um . . . *you?*' said Woody. 'Sorry, I've completely forgotten your name.'

'Liam,' said Liam. 'My sister's Sarah.'

'Oh yes, I remember now,' said Woody. 'Sorry, I've got a terrible memory for names.'

'Can we maybe have this conversation *after* you've stopped me turning into a shrubbery?' Jake snapped. 'My fingernails are going green!'

'Step aside . . . sorry, it's gone again,' said Woody.

'Liam.'

'Liam! Yes. Sorry. Step aside, Liam,' said Woody. He marched into the greenhouse, swinging in a wide arc with the axe. Jake's whole body stiffened as the blade came swishing towards his head. He screwed his eyes shut and braced himself for the—

THWACK!

Jake opened one eye, then the other. The vines fell from the top of his head, and he was able to look around. Woody had prised open a wooden panel at

108

the top of the chair, revealing a spaghetti of wires and several rusted buttons inside. The chair shuddered as Woody hammered at the buttons, then the vines around Jake's arms slithered back into the woodwork. Woody caught Jake by the arm and dragged him to safety.

'Woody! Am I glad you're here!' Jake wheezed. He rubbed his wrists for a moment. 'But why are you here?'

'I come in every Saturday,' Woody said.

Liam gasped and clutched at his chest. 'To school? Are you mad?'

'The plants need watering,' Woody explained. 'Plus, I find it easier to get work done without everyone else around.'

Jake reached under the leaves of a plant and picked Max up. He growled deep down in his throat, until Jake stroked him on the top of his head to calm him. 'It's OK, it's just Woody,' Jake reassured his dog.

'What about you two?' Woody asked. 'What's going on?'

Jake and Liam looked at one another, then both began babbling at once.

'There's a big plant monster ...'

'We think it's Mr Campion ...'

'Possibly working with Professor Bloom ...'

'Even though she's probably dead ...'

'We found her hand . . .'

'We think . . .'

'And then saw the Creeper cut his off . . .'

'Only it grew back . . .'

Woody's head tick-tocked left and right, like a spectator at a tennis match. His expression grew more amazed as he listened to Jake and Liam's story unfold.

'The Creeper?' Woody said, raising an eyebrow.

'Yes, that's the name we've given to the monster,' Jake said. 'We saw him in here along with this . . .'

Jake paused, mid-way through gesturing to the potato-man. Slowly, his gaze shifted to Woody. For the first time, he noticed a bright red mark on Woody's cheek, right where he'd hit the Creeper with the salt.

'You didn't ask about this thing,' Jake said.

Woody looked the potato-man up and down. 'Oh. Yes,' he said. 'I didn't notice it.'

Liam snorted. 'You didn't notice a full-sized adult with the body of a potato standing a metre in front of you? I thought you science types were meant to be really observant.'

Jake took a step back. 'Uh, Liam.'

'I mean, how could you not notice?' Liam continued.

'Liam . . .'

Liam laughed. 'It's almost like you already knew . . .' His voice trailed off. He cleared his throat gently. 'You already knew it was here.'

'That burn on your face,' said Jake. 'How did you get it?'

For a moment, Woody looked like he was going to deny any knowledge of the burn on his face, but then his expression darkened and he tightened his grip on the axe. 'I was *assaulted*.'

'Hey,' Liam protested weakly. 'That was my joke.'

'You caught me off guard with your little salt attack. Forced me to change back,' Woody hissed. 'Temporarily,' he added, threateningly.

'You're the Creeper, not Mr Campion,' Jake realized. 'And you killed Professor Bloom!'

'Oh, don't be ridiculous,' said a voice from the doorway. Everyone turned to find a stocky woman with scraped-back hair standing there, her hands on her hips. *Both* hands. 'Do I look like I'm dead to you?'

Jake and Liam's jaws dropped. Even Max looked shocked.

'Professor Bloom? You're alive!' said Jake.

Liam scratched his head. 'She's alive?'

'She's alive,' Woody confirmed.

'Yes, I'm alive,' agreed the professor. 'I think we can safely say we've established that now.'

Jake's mouth flapped open and closed. He looked from Professor Bloom to Woody, then back again.

'So ... But ... I mean ...'

Professor Bloom laughed. It was a dry scrape at the back of her throat, and not like a real laugh at all. 'You have questions, of course. Don't worry, I'll answer them,' she said. A wicked smile crept across her face. 'After all, my plan is already well under way.'

Something sinister glinted behind her eyes. 'And there's not a thing you can do to stop me!'

CHAPTER TWELVE

THE PLAN REVEALED

Back in the lab, Sarah crawled out from under the desk. She'd heard two sets of footsteps pass through the classroom a few minutes apart. She could hear voices from out in the garden now—one of which should have been impossible.

'Professor Bloom,' Sarah whispered, peeking out through the lab's back door. She was about to step out when she spotted the expressions on Jake and Liam's faces. They weren't just surprised to see the professor in one piece, they were scared.

Sarah tucked herself into the corner beside the door and strained her ears as she tried to listen in on the conversation outside.

'What plan?' Jake asked. 'What are you going to do?'

Professor Bloom gave a dismissive wave. 'All in good time,' she said.

'But . . . you're definitely not dead, though?' asked Liam.

'Definitely,' said Professor Bloom.

'Right.' Liam nodded. 'And were you dead at any point?'

'No.'

'Gotcha. Carry on.'

Professor Bloom nodded. 'You see—'

'Wait,' said Liam, interrupting her. 'Whose hand was it?'

'Mine,' said Woody.

Jake and Liam looked at Woody's hands, which seemed to be completely intact.

'Oh. Right,' said Liam. 'That makes much more sense.'

Professor Bloom glared at the boys. 'Can I carry on now? Are we quite finished?'

Liam mimed zipping his mouth shut and gave her a nod.

'I pretended to be sick so I could work on my plan at home, away from the prying eyes of the other teachers—and meddling pupils,' the professor said. 'You see, I was planning something so awful, so utterly, unforgivably terrible, that I couldn't risk anyone finding out about it before I was ready.'

'Like us, you mean,' said Jake.

Professor Bloom laughed sharply. 'Well, yes, except for two minor points—one, you don't know anything about my plan, and two . . . ' She reached into her pocket and pulled out her mobile phone just as it let out a series of shrill bleeps. 'I *am* ready.'

She silenced the phone alarm, then turned sharply towards the door. She skipped out into the garden, more animated and excited than Jake had ever seen her in class. Woody gave the boys a shove with the axe handle, and they stumbled into the garden behind the teacher.

'So . . . I don't get it,' said Liam.

'Which bit?' Jake asked.

'All of it,' Liam admitted.

'Behold!' cried Professor Bloom, before Jake could answer. She spread her arms in the direction of her vegetable patch. The ground was churning and shaking, just like it had done back at her house. 'They're ready!'

'Who's ready?' asked Jake, as Max, in his arms, began to bark again.

'They are!' cried the professor. She pointed to the trembling soil.

Nothing happened.

'Give it a minute,' she said, slightly less dramatically.

Her finger was still stretched out, pointing. 'Any second
. . . now. No, now. Wait. Nnnnnnnnnnnooooooooow.'

'There,' said Woody, pointing to another patch of
dirt just a metre or so away. Jake and Liam both gasped
as four fat worms pushed up from beneath the ground.
It wasn't until the fifth one emerged that they realized
they weren't worms at all.

They were fingers.

All across the vegetable patch, more hands began to
emerge, sprouting up out of the muddy soil like plants
growing towards the sun.

'Zombies!' Liam cried.

'Don't be ludicrous,' Professor Bloom sneered.
'They're genetically engineered potato-men!'

'Oh yeah,' Jake muttered, 'because that's far less
ridiculous.'

He and Liam both tried to step back as the potato-
people dragged themselves up out of the ground, but
Woody blocked their escape.

The spud-folk looked much like the one that was
currently unmoving in the greenhouse, only their eyes
were bulgier, their arms were thicker, and their bodies
were a little less lumpy and misshapen.

'Aren't they wonderful?' Professor Bloom whispered.

'*Golden* Wonderful,' said Liam. He looked at Jake
and grinned. 'See what I did there? Golden Wonder is

116

a type of potato,' he explained.

'Really not the time,' Jake told him.

'No, probably not,' Liam admitted. 'Good joke, though.'

Jake shrugged. 'Meh.'

'These are my children,' Professor Bloom announced.

'They must get their looks from their dad,' said Liam.

The teacher shot him an irritated look, then continued. 'I grew them from seedlings. Seedlings I had manipulated at the genetic level to become something far more than the average potato!'

'You can say that again,' said Jake, looking the hulking figures up and down. There were five of them, all standing in a line behind Professor Bloom, their bulbous eyes watching her every move.

'And now, perhaps, my plan becomes clear!' said the professor.

Jake and Liam shot each other a glance. 'Not really,' confessed Jake. 'I still don't really have a clue what you're on about.'

'Yeah,' agreed Liam. 'I'm still trying to get my head round the fact you're alive.' He pointed to the potato-men. 'What have Lumpy, Bumpy, Dumpy, and . . . those other two I can't think of names for, got to do with anything?'

117

'You've given potatoes legs,' said Jake. 'How is that an evil plan?'

Professor Bloom seethed. 'Because they're going to use those legs to march across the face of the Earth, you idiots! With me as their leader.'

Jake let out a single loud, 'Ha!' He shook his head. 'I don't think the army will have much trouble fighting five—admittedly quite large—potatoes.'

'Not just large,' Professor Bloom said. 'Lethal. Deadly. Every one of them a genetically engineered killing machine.' She flexed her fingers, cricked her neck, and grinned. 'Oh, and *me*.'

Jake and Liam looked her up and down. 'What are

you going to do?' Liam asked. 'Give all the soldiers detention?'

Professor Bloom rocked back on her heels. 'No. I'm going to mutate my own DNA, turning me into an unstoppable part-human, part-plant creature, and then I'll tear them all apart.'

Liam swallowed. His smirk fell away. 'Yeah, that was going to be my second guess.'

Jake scratched his head. 'So . . . are you the Creeper, then?' he asked. 'Or is the monster Woody?'

'Or is it Mr Campion? Because that's who I thought it was,' Liam said. 'Also, just to be clear, you're *definitely* not dead?'

'It isn't *a monster*,' Professor Bloom spat. 'It's art. It's evolution. It's the future!'

'It's a freaky big plant-thing with glowing eyes,' said Jake. 'Makes it a monster in my book.'

Professor Bloom took a sudden step closer, and for a moment Jake thought she was going to hit him. Instead, she just leaned over him and smiled, showing her yellow teeth. 'Bring them,' she ordered Woody. 'Bring them both. They shall witness my rebirth!'

The teacher rolled up her sleeves as she marched back into the greenhouse. Woody shoved the boys along behind her.

'It's simple, really,' Bloom began. 'I created a device designed to splice the genetic code of plants with that of humans. Plants are so versatile, much more so than our rather pathetic flesh and blood. Of course, I couldn't possibly test it on myself, so I needed someone less important to experiment on. Someone disposable.'

She glanced back at her assistant. 'That's where Woody came in. He resisted at first, of course, but once he'd had a taste of the power my machine could give him, he soon became my willing slave.'

'Assistant,' Woody corrected.

Professor Bloom scowled at him. 'Same thing.'

Jake peered out through the greenhouse's dirty glass. The potato-men had formed a semicircle around the doorway, blocking any chance of escape. On the one hand, they looked quite ridiculous, but on the other, they were up there with the most terrifying things he'd ever seen, second only to the Creeper himself.

For a moment, Jake thought he saw movement behind the spud-people, back in the doorway of the lab, but the glass was too dirty for him to tell for sure.

The wooden throne creaked as Professor Bloom lowered herself into it. 'Now, my machine is perfect, just like my latest batch of potato-men,' she said.

Woody patted the statue-like potato figure on the shoulder. 'I can probably get this prototype going again, too,' he said. 'Just needs some fine-tuning.'

Professor Bloom turned in the chair and tapped a few buttons in the control panel mounted into the back. Vines and branches grew from the chair and wrapped around the teacher's limbs, just like they'd done to Jake. Where Jake had been terrified, though, Professor Bloom's face was twisted with glee.

'Now, once Woody activates it, I will be transformed—reborn as something better. Something more! I shall become the first true human–plant hybrid!'

'Second,' Woody reminded her.

'You?' snorted the professor. She nodded in the direction of the frozen spud-man. 'You're merely a prototype, like that useless lump. I, on the other hand, will be the real thing, and I will rule the world!'

'We,' said Woody. 'You said that we would rule the world.'

'Don't be ridiculous,' Professor Bloom said. 'I will rule, you will obey, just the way it has always been. Now hurry up and pour in the genetic material, so I can evolve!'

Woody took a step closer to the machine, then stopped. He looked down at the axe, still held tightly in both hands. For a moment, Jake thought he was going to chop the teacher's head off, but instead he bent and propped it up against a bag of fertilizer.

He interlocked his fingers and flexed them out in front of him until the knuckles went *crack*.

'Hurry up, you fool,' Professor Bloom spat. 'Begin the transformation!'

Woody shrugged. 'OK,' he said. 'If you insist.'

Everyone watched as Woody held his hands up in front of him, fingers splayed. A little white sprout grew from the tip of one thumb. It snaked and curled in the air, like a worm feeling its way.

'What?' Professor Bloom gasped. 'How is that possible? How are you doing that without the chair?'

'It's like you said, professor,' said Woody. He grinned, showing teeth that had become rough and brown like the bark of a tree. 'I've evolved. I don't need your machine any more. I can transform all by myself.'

He opened his mouth fully and moss spread out from inside like a rash. It rushed across his face, replacing his skin. His fleshy arms hardened and twisted into thick branches. His mud-stained overalls ripped, as row after row of thorns grew from his suddenly much broader back.

'The power!' he cried, his voice like the creaking of an old oak tree. 'Such unbelievable power!'

His green eyes flashed angrily at Professor Bloom. 'You think you can take this away from me? You think you can rob me of my rightful place as ruler?'

'Cut it out, Woody,' Professor Bloom scowled. 'Behave yourself! That's an order.'

Woody shuddered with delight as those tentacle-like vines grew from his back and snapped at the air. 'You have no idea how it feels,' he told the teacher. One of his tentacles stabbed into the throne, piercing deep into the wood. 'And you never will!'

The chair began to vibrate violently. Professor Bloom's eyes widened in panic as she struggled against her bonds. 'What? What are you doing? Stop this, Woody! Stop this right now!'

'Sorry, Woody doesn't live here any more,' he hissed through his mossy lips. 'You can call me the Creeper!'

'We should have totally trademarked that,' Liam whispered, but Jake was too transfixed by what was happening to Professor Bloom to hear him.

The chair was pulling her in, almost like it was absorbing her into the surface of the wood. She screamed as her arms and legs seemed to retreat into her body, then the scream became a gurgle, and the gurgle became a soft, soggy *squelch*.

Jake and Liam both stared at the throne. All that was left of Professor Bloom was a small mound of mulchy soil.

Liam looked at the chair. He looked at Jake. 'So *now* she's dead, right?'

'Yes,' said Jake, swallowing hard. 'Now she's definitely dead.'

The Creeper let out a *burp*, then withdrew his vine from the chair. 'Excuse me,' the Creeper said. 'I just ate something that didn't agree with me.'

'You *ate* her?' Jake gasped.

The Creeper gazed curiously at his tentacle. 'Yes. It appears I did,' he said. 'How interesting.'

'By "interesting" do you mean "mind-bogglingly revolting"?' Liam asked, but the Creeper ignored him.

The throne was still shaking and shuddering, the movements growing more and more violent with each second that passed. Behind it, two panes of glass were

124

shaken loose. They smashed against the floor just as the chair began to grow. Its roots plunged deeper into the ground. Branches extended upwards, punching through the roof windows and showering Jake and Liam with yet more glass.

'What have you done?' Jake demanded.

'I've set the machine to self-destruct,' the Creeper told them. 'I wouldn't want anyone else getting this power, would I?'

He placed a hand on the statue-like potato-man and frowned in concentration. A moment later, the frozen figure blinked its bulbous eyes, as if waking from a trance, then immediately turned and stepped outside to stand with the others.

'I knew I could fix him. Another loyal soldier to join my ranks,' crowed the Creeper. He locked Jake and Liam with a blazing, green-eyed stare. 'And those are just the beginning!'

CHAPTER THIRTEEN

MAN VS FOOD

'You were right, you know,' said the Creeper. 'I can't possibly take over the world with just a handful of soldiers.'

'Exactly. So you might as well give up now,' said Jake.

The Creeper smirked. 'Nice try.' He gestured to the small vegetable patch, which was now filled with man-sized holes. The potato-men were lined up, three on each side of it.

'Amazing, isn't it?' said the Creeper. 'Five fully-grown specimens out of one tiny plot of land. Imagine what I could do with, oh, I don't know, a full-sized football pitch.'

'Ha! Well you're out of luck, moss-features' said

Liam. 'We don't have a football pitch any more, it's been turned into a big field!'

'Exactly!' said the Creeper.

Liam nodded. 'Exactly yourself.' He glanced sideways at Jake. 'What's he saying "exactly" for?'

Jake rolled his eyes. 'Because he turned the football field into one big vegetable plot,' Jake said. 'And we helped him plant it.'

It took a moment for Liam to understand, but then his face contorted in horror. 'What? So . . . those potatoes we planted are going to turn into those things?'

'Yep,' said Jake. He turned to the Creeper. 'That's right, isn't it?'

'Precisely,' said the Creeper. 'You literally sowed the seeds of your own destruction, and didn't even realize you were doing it,' he said.

'So Mr Campion *is* a bad guy, after all!' said Liam. 'Or is he? I'll be honest, I'm a little confused.'

'Mr Campion is a prattling buffoon,' said the Creeper.

'Oh yeah, we know that,' said Jake. 'But is he an *evil* prattling buffoon, or just a bog-standard normal one?'

Two of the Creeper's vines snaked into the ground. A moment later the hedge ahead of them parted like a pair of theatre curtains. Through the gap, they could see the enormous patch of dirt that had once been the football field.

The Creeper started to make his way towards it. Behind him, the potato-men flanked Jake and Liam, forcing them to follow in the monster's footsteps.

'I tricked him into it,' the Creeper said. 'It was ridiculously easy to make him think planting the potatoes was all his idea. For a head teacher, he really is quite remarkably dim.'

Jake and Liam weren't really listening. They were, instead, staring in amazement at the way the Creeper was travelling across the grass. He wasn't moving his legs; instead, the individual blades of grass seemed to be passing him between each other, carrying him towards his destination. It was like a crowd-surfer at a concert, only much more impressive.

They arrived at the former football pitch and the Creeper stepped onto the soil. His whole body shuddered, and fresh shoots sprouted from his limbs and torso. 'Can you feel it?' he whispered. 'The power of nature. The power of plants. It radiates from the soil itself, making me stronger, faster, better. And she thought she could rob me of it. The fool.'

He spun on the spot, flailing his arms and tendrils around him. 'This world belongs to me, and I belong to it. The human race is a disease. A pest. Like greenfly.'

128

He stopped spinning and fixed the boys with a wicked stare. 'And you know what we do to greenfly, don't you?'

'Let them off with a warning and send them home?' asked Liam, hopefully.

The Creeper shook his head. 'I'm afraid not.'

Jake and Liam huddled together as the potato-men turned towards them. Max gave a couple of barks, which turned into growls, then whimpers, as twelve branch-like arms reached out to grab the boys and the dog.

'Back off, veg-heads!' Liam warned. He flapped his arms around in front of him, in what he hoped was a threatening way. 'I know karate or kung fu, or that other one where you wear the big skirt, and I'm not afraid to use it!'

'Kill them,' instructed the Creeper. 'Kill them both.'

Suddenly, the ground began to rumble. Jake and Liam both looked down, expecting to see the soil churning, but it was completely still. The potato-men's pudgy faces frowned. Even the Creeper looked confused.

A horn blasted. Jake and Liam spun in time to see a tractor thundering towards them across the grass, Sarah bouncing around in the seat.

'Look out!' she warned.

Jake and Liam hurled themselves sideways just as the tractor hurtled past. The thick, iron grille on the front slammed into two of the potato-men. They exploded like gunge-filled balloons, spraying gooey strands of wet potato in all directions.

'Quick,' called Sarah, turning in the seat. 'Jump on!'

The tractor was already bouncing across the ploughed field. Jake and Liam dodged past the potato-men, avoided the Creeper, then went racing after the retreating farm vehicle.

The Creeper scooped a big blob of potato-man off his face and flicked it onto the ground. 'Get them!' he growled. 'Get them and bring them all to me!'

The potato-men didn't need to be told twice. They set off after Jake, Liam, and the tractor, waddling from side to side as they ran. Ahead of them, Liam jumped onto the back of the tractor, then reached down to pull Jake and Max aboard.

'Not bad, sis,' Liam grinned, when they were all safely huddled up on the tractor's bench-like seat. 'Not bad at all.'

'You didn't think I was going to let you two have all the fun, did you? Grab those,' said Sarah, nodding towards a rake and a shovel which were hooked onto the side of the tractor.

Jake tucked Max safely into the footwell, then took

the rake and passed Liam the shovel. 'What are these for?' Liam asked.

Jake gave the rake an experimental swish. 'Ever made mashed potato?' he asked.

Liam shook his head. 'No.'

'Well, now's your chance,' said Sarah. She yanked sharply on the steering wheel and the tractor skidded around in a half-circle, then came to a stop.

The four remaining potato-men were bounding towards them. The way their lumpy bodies wobbled with every step almost made them look comical, but Jake knew there was nothing funny about them.

'Shouldn't we, you know, phone the police?' said Liam.

Sarah revved the engine. 'They didn't believe us when we said we found a hand,' she reminded him. 'How do you think they'll react when we say we're fighting genetically engineered potato-men?'

Liam thought about this. 'With surprise?' he guessed.

'They won't believe us. They won't come,' said Sarah. 'Which means we've got to do this on our own.'

'You heard what the Creeper said. If they catch us they'll kill us,' said Liam.

Jake twirled the rake in his hands, then gripped the long wooden handle tightly. 'Then we won't let

131

them catch us,' he said. He gave Sarah a nod and she slammed her foot to the floor. The tractor rolled forwards slowly. It wasn't nearly as dramatic as Jake would have liked, but then the vehicle hadn't really been built for speed.

'You take your side, I'll take my side,' Jake told Liam.

'And I'll hit anything in the middle,' said Sarah. She rocked in her seat, trying to make the tractor go faster.

'You're enjoying this!' Liam yelped.

Sarah smirked. 'Little bit,' she admitted.

SPLAT! One of the spud-people hit the front of the tractor and exploded, splattering against the front windscreen.

'One potato!' Sarah called.

Liam screamed as another of the creatures made a grab for his leg. Panicking, he kicked it away, then brought the spade down hard on its head, mashing it down into its squidgy body.

'Two potato!' he yelped.

Jake swung with the rake at another of the potato-men. The metal prongs dug into the brute's skin. Its already bulging eyes almost doubled in size as Jake yanked on the rake, pulling the creature under the tractor's wheels.

'Three potato!' he cheered.

SLAM! The last remaining spud-creature hurled itself onto the back of the tractor and hammered its fists against the rear windscreen.

'Four!' gulped Liam.

'Shake him off!' Jake cried.

Sarah turned the wheel. The tractor bounced through the muddy soil, but the potato-man held on.

'Turn faster!' Liam yelped.

'I can't! It's a tractor, not a sports car,' Sarah pointed out. She yanked the wheel sharply right. The tractor weaved sideways and the potato-man slid left across the glass. For a moment, it looked like it might go tumbling off, but then one of its arms reached round and made a grab for the steering wheel.

'Let go!' Sarah cried, wrestling with the wheel. The potato-man was much stronger than she was, though, and was easily turning the tractor around, steering them back towards the Creeper.

Liam and Jake both heaved, and hammered, and hit out at the arm, but it was like trying to fight a tree trunk.

'It's too strong!' Jake groaned. 'It's no use!'

From down in the footwell came an angry growl. Max leaped up onto the seat between Jake and Sarah, bared his teeth, then chomped down hard on the potato-man's arm. The creature let out an inhuman

133

squeal and released its grip on the wheel. It pulled its arm out of the cab, Max still hanging on by his little jaws.

'Liam, the head! Go for the head!' Jake said, spinning in his seat.

'Which bit's the head?!' Liam shouted, turning the other way. He swung with his spade just as Jake did the same with his rake. The implements smashed into the potato-creature on either side, then gave a muffled *clank* as they met in the middle.

The misshapen body exploded, spraying the back windscreen with mushy goo. Max fell to the ground, still holding the creature's arm between his teeth. It now looked like nothing more than a big stick. Max's tail wagged happily as he trotted along with his prize in his mouth.

'Yeah!' cheered Liam. 'We roasted those spuds!'

'We mashed them right up!' laughed Jake.

'We sautéed them!' added Sarah. The boys looked at her, puzzled. She sighed. 'It's a way of cooking potatoes that involves chopping them up, part-boiling them for a few minutes, then frying them.'

Liam shook his head. 'You made it far too complicated,' he told her.

Sarah tutted. 'Alright, fine. We baked them, then. Is that better?'

Liam wrinkled his nose. 'Not really.'

'Doesn't really make sense,' Jake agreed.

Sarah scowled. 'I hate you two, sometimes.'

She brought the tractor rumbling to a stop. The Creeper stood in the centre of the field, his gaze sweeping across the mushy remains of his potato creations.

'He doesn't look very happy,' said Liam.

'No,' said Jake.

'Mind you, his face is mostly made of twigs, so it's hard to tell.'

'Yeah,' said Jake.

'What do we do now?' Sarah asked.

'Now we go to the police,' said Jake.

Sarah and Liam both frowned. 'But we talked about that.' said Sarah. 'They won't believe us.'

'They will now,' Jake said. He held up his mobile phone and flicked through the photos. They showed the picture he'd taken of the Creeper in the greenhouse, and several snaps of the potato-men attacking the tractor. 'Thought I should grab some evidence,' he said, grinning.

He and Liam exchanged a high five, then Jake leaned out of the tractor cab. 'You've lost, Creeper. We've beaten your spud-buddies, and the rest of them are still six feet under. It's over. You might as well give up.'

135

The Creeper's green eyes narrowed. 'Give up?' he hissed. His shoulders shook as he began to chuckle. He threw back his spiky head, and his laughter rolled across the field towards them. 'Oh, you poor, deluded child,' the Creeper said.

The vines on his back all burrowed, one by one, into the soil at his feet. 'It isn't *over*,' the monster cried. 'Why, it's barely even begun!'

The tractor shuddered. The ground trembled.

From one end of the field to the other, the soil began to roll and churn. The Creeper raised his arms to the sky in triumph as, all around him, hands clawed up from the earth below.

'Uh-oh,' Jake whispered. 'Looks like his reinforcements are ready.'

CHAPTER FOURTEEN

A BUMPER CROP

The whole field heaved and squirmed with bodies as they pulled themselves up out of the ground. Ten potato-men dragged themselves upright. Twenty. Fifty. Soon, the whole field was full of them, all bent and misshapen—and all turning towards the tractor.

'There must be a hundred of them,' said Jake.

'More like two hundred,' Sarah guessed.

'We only just managed to beat six of them,' Liam said, his voice little more than a high-pitched squeak of terror. 'How are we meant to fight two hundred?'

Suddenly, a hand shot out of the ground right beside the tractor. It clamped onto the side step and pulled hard. The whole vehicle rocked sideways, forcing them to grab onto the door-frames to stop

themselves falling out.

'Go, go, go!' Jake cried.

Sarah stamped a foot down on the accelerator. The big back wheels spun, churning up a spray of soil and mud, but the tractor didn't move. On all sides, the potato-men began to close in.

'You're not going!' Liam pointed out. 'Why aren't you going?'

'It's stuck!' Sarah hissed through gritted teeth. She eased off the pedal then pushed it to the floor again. The wheels squealed as they churned up another cloud of dirt. 'It's the hand! Get rid of the hand!'

Jake slammed the metal end of the rake down across the potato-thing's knotty knuckles. Once. Twice. Again. Again!

He raised the rake for a fifth time, but the thing's mangled fingers lost their grip, and the tractor sped forwards with a sudden lurch of power. Jake slipped off the seat and plunged towards the ground below. Sarah dived for him, catching him by the belt of his jeans.

'Ow! Wedgie, wedgie!' Jake yelped.

'Liam, take the wheel,' Sarah barked.

'Where do you want me to—?'

'And *no jokes*!' Sarah growled.

She slid over in the seat, her arms straining as she fought to pull Jake back into the cab. Liam gave the wheel a sudden turn, and Sarah almost tumbled out, too.

'Watch what you're doing!' Sarah cried.

'I was avoiding a potato-guy!' Liam protested.

'Well don't! Hit as many as you can,' Sarah said. She let out a cry of effort as she heaved Jake back onto the tractor.

'Thanks,' Jake wheezed.

'Wow,' said Liam. 'You're stronger than you look.'

'And don't you forget it!' Sarah warned him, nudging him out of the way and taking the wheel again. She spun it sharply, aiming for the closest of the potato-men. This new batch were smarter than the others, though, and the creature simply side-stepped out of the tractor's path.

Not all the potato-men were the same, this time. Most of them looked pretty much like the last lot, but a few of them were bigger. Much bigger. They towered almost as tall as the tractor, with arms and legs like the branches of ancient oak trees.

One of the giant potato-creatures raised an arm. It pointed a twig-like finger at the tractor. There was a *pop*, which was followed almost immediately by the sound of shattering glass as the back windscreen exploded.

Jake and the others ducked, covering their heads

with their hands.

'What was that?' Jake cried.

Liam rummaged in the broken glass and held up a small rectangle of hard-packed potato. 'It's a spud gun! That big one tried to shoot us with a spud gun!' he announced, then he pulled a disgusted face. 'Which is like trying to shoot us with its own guts! These things are monsters!'

'You don't say,' Sarah muttered. She swerved again, trying to mash through a tightly-packed group of the creatures, but they dived for safety and she missed them all by several centimetres. 'Argh, stop jumping out of the way!' she cried.

'I doubt they're going to agree to that,' Liam said.

POP! Another spud pellet whistled through the air beside the tractor.

CLANK! Another hit the wheel arch, denting it.

'They're just like real bullets. If those things hit us, we're done for!' Jake said.

'Pretty sure we're done for, anyway,' Sarah said. She turned the tractor in a wide circle, avoiding a squad of spud-people who had been approaching from the left.

'We could just drive right through them,' Liam suggested. 'Keep going straight and don't turn for anything.'

There was a loud BANG from not too far away,

as the greenhouse finally shook itself to pieces. The wooden throne—or machine, as Professor Bloom and the Creeper had called it—was still shuddering and vibrating. It sounded like it might blow up at any moment.

'But don't go that way,' Liam advised. 'That does not sound healthy.'

'Don't worry, I'm not completely barking mad,' Sarah told him.

Jake gasped. *Barking*.

'Max!' he cried, spinning in the seat and searching the ground around them. 'Where's Max?'

'You've lost him again?' said Liam. 'You are *such* an irresponsible pet owner.'

'There!' Sarah said, pointing over to their right. Max was snapping and snarling at one of the larger potato-men. Its bulging, bloodshot eyes peered down at him, like it couldn't quite work out what this noisy little creature was trying to do.

'Max, no! Here, boy!' Jake called.

Max kept barking and growling. The potato-creature opened its enormous hand and slowly reached down.

'Max, please! Come on!'

The hair on the little dog's back was all bunched up and standing on end. His opponent might have been

143

several hundred times his size, and made of mutated potato, but Max was ready for a fight.

'It's no use,' Liam said. 'He's not going to listen.'

'I've got cake!' Jake cried.

Max stopped barking. He turned his head. He licked his lips. Then, with a twitch of his back legs, he sped across the field, leaving a trail of churned-up mud in his wake.

'Except to that, obviously,' said Liam. 'Ah, cake. Is there nothing it can't do?'

When Max was halfway to the tractor, the giant potato-man formed his hand into a gun-shape. Jake's eyes went wide with horror as the monster took aim.

'Max, look out!' he cried, but it was too late.

There was a POP.

There was a YELP.

And Max rolled, head over tail, through the dirt, then tumbled to a stop.

'No!' Jake cried. He leaped down from the tractor, his rake clutched in both hands.

'Jake! Jake, don't, it's too dangerous!' Sarah called after him, but nothing was going to stop Jake reaching his dog.

A potato-man lunged for him, but Jake dodged back and swung with his rake as hard as he could. He struck the creature, knocking its top half clean off.

Immediately, it collapsed into a fluffy white mush.

Another spud-creature approached from behind. Jake stabbed the rake's long wooden handle backwards, driving it deep into the thing's soft flesh. The potato-man let out a low gurgle, then folded in on itself like a collapsing soufflé.

Jake twirled around, flicking the rake out in a wide circle. Two more potato-people went down hard, splattering into squidgy goo when they hit the ground.

But Jake wasn't there to fight. He dodged past another few outstretched arms, ducked under a pair of branch-like legs, then scrambled across to the unmoving Max.

'Please don't be dead, please don't be dead,' Jake whispered, hot tears stinging at his eyes. The dog's body was limp and motionless. There was a lump poking through a patch of bare fur, where the spud bullet had grazed Max's head. Despite the monsters closing in on all sides, Jake burrowed his head in against the dog's fur and hugged Max closely.

'Oh, Max, I'm sorry!' he said, his voice cracking. 'I never should have brought you.'

Something rough and wet slobbered in his ear. Jake leaned back in surprise to find Max's head turned to look at him. The dog let out a weak whine and

145

glanced at Jake's pocket, as if to say, *So, about that cake you mentioned . . . ?*

'Max! You're alive,' Jake gasped. 'You're alive!'

'For now,' spat an all-too-familiar voice from behind them. Jake got to his feet, holding the dog close to his chest. He turned, and came face to face with the Creeper. A twisted smile lit up the monster's mossy face. 'You were saying something earlier about it being over . . .'

'Why are you doing this?' Jake asked, shooting nervous glances at the potato-people. They were gathered in a circle around him and the Creeper, like they were getting ready to watch a fight. Jake knew there was no way he could fight this monster, though. Not without a few bags of salt, at least. And, ideally, a flamethrower. 'What have we ever done to you?'

'It's not about what you've done to me,' the Creeper snarled. 'It's about what we have done to the plants.'

He waved his hand and the grass rippled, carrying him closer to Jake. 'Since man first walked upright, we've done nothing but abuse the flora of this world,' the Creeper said. 'We've cut down trees. We've picked flowers. We've plucked and torn and chopped and scythed without pity. Without remorse.'

Jake wanted to say, *yeah, but they're just plants*, but

146

decided it probably wasn't the best time, and so kept his mouth shut.

'I have always felt a kinship with them. A connection,' continued the Creeper. 'My childhood was not a happy one. I didn't have many friends, but I had my plants to tend and water and care for. They needed me.'

The Creeper's green eyes flashed brighter. 'And they need me now, more than ever.'

'For what?' asked Jake. He glanced around, searching for a way through the potato-men, but they were bunched too tightly together.

'For revenge!' cried the Creeper, his voice rolling like thunder across the field. 'For justice! Too long has mankind trampled and harvested my brothers and sisters. Too long have the plants been mistreated and abused.'

'He wasn't that fussed about harvesting his brothers and sisters when he was feeding the throne,' Jake muttered.

The Creeper threw his arms into the air, gesturing around them. 'Long before mankind first crawled out of its primordial swamp, the world belonged to us.' The Creeper's mossy face split into a grin. 'Today, we're taking it back. And there's nothing you can do to stop—'

147

WHAM! The tractor slammed into the Creeper from the side, sending him hurtling into the crowd of potato-men.

'Hurry, get on!' Sarah yelped.

Jake passed Max up to Liam, then scrambled onto the tractor. Sarah floored the accelerator and the vehicle lurched across the mud, scattering more of the potato-creatures, who instinctively parted to avoid being crushed.

'Thought you could do with a bit of help,' said Sarah.

'Thanks,' Jake replied. 'I was pretty scared back there.'

Liam waved a hand in front of his face and wrinkled his nose. 'So I can smell. That's rotten, mate.'

Jake frowned. 'What?'

'Was that just a fart, or did you follow through?' Liam asked, pulling his t-shirt up over his mouth. 'Either way, I think you need to see a doctor.'

Jake started to protest, then he smelled it, too. 'Wait . . .' he said, sniffing the air. 'That's gas.'

'Well, that's a relief,' said Liam. 'I thought you'd actually cacked your pants.'

'No, I mean proper gas, from the gas main,' said Jake.

Sarah sniffed, too. 'You're right.' She looked ahead

148

to Professor Bloom's garden. The throne had now mutated into a tangle of branches, vines, and roots, and was shuddering violently. Smoke curled up from within it, as if the machine was going to catch fire at any moment. 'The roots must have smashed through a gas pipe. It could blow at any second!'

'We have to get out of here,' Jake cried. Sarah started to turn the wheel, but Liam clamped a hand on her wrist.

'Wait!' he whispered. His eyes narrowed and darted from side to side, as if reading something inside his own head. 'I think ... I think ... Yep,' he said, and Jake could practically see a lightbulb appear above his head. 'I've just had an idea.'

'Is it stupid and dangerous?' Sarah asked.

Liam nodded. 'Yep.'

Sarah and Jake both exchanged a look. They shrugged.

'OK, then,' said Jake. 'Count us in.'

Sarah ploughed towards the potato-men on the tractor, Liam and Jake both holding on to the door-frame on either side. Max was curled up on the floor, still dazed from the spud pellet.

The Creeper was back on his feet now. He stood in the middle of his starchy creations, glaring at the approaching farm vehicle.

'Are you sure about this?' Sarah whispered.

'Definitely,' said Liam. 'I've done it before.'

Sarah and Jake both blinked in surprise. 'How can you have done it before?' Jake asked.

'Well, not exactly the same,' Liam admitted. 'But I've done similar. You see, the plan's based on something in *Brick-Quest*.'

'What?!' Sarah yelped. She slammed on the brakes. 'I've changed my mind. Forget this plan.'

'It's the only one we've got,' Jake reminded her. 'If we don't stop the Creeper he's going to destroy everything. We have to try.'

Sarah groaned. She crunched the tractor into gear and started moving again. 'We are so going to die.'

The tractor drew closer to the potato-men. 'Now?' Sarah asked.

'Not yet,' Liam urged. 'Bit closer.'

The tractor trundled another few metres across the soil. 'Now?'

'Bit closer . . .'

'We can't get much closer!' Sarah said. 'We're about to run out of—'

'Now!'

Sarah yanked the wheel and hammered the brake at the same time, sending the tractor into a skid. It spun 180 degrees, so it was now facing away from the

Creeper and his potato army.

Liam and Jake looked at each other and nodded. 'Let's do this,' said Jake.

They both turned and leaned out of the tractor. 'Hey, you know what I could go for right now?' Liam shouted. 'A nice big baked potato.'

'Mmm,' said Jake. 'All mashed up with butter.'

'Or just mash, actually,' added Liam. 'Picture it, Jake, just a big steaming bowl of fluffy mash. Imagine tucking into that.'

'Yum!' said Jake, rubbing his stomach.

The potato-people began to shamble forwards, but hesitantly. The Creeper's face darkened.

'Stay where you are,' he told his minions. 'They're up to something.'

'Not really, just thinking about lunch,' Jake said, shrugging. 'Roast potatoes might be nice.'

The potato-men shuffled angrily.

'Or chips,' suggested Liam.

The potato-men cracked their knotty knuckles.

'Or sautéed!' Sarah called.

The potato-men frowned. Sarah tutted. 'You boil them first, then get a frying pan . . .'

'I told you, it's too complicated,' Liam sighed. He looked back at the potato army and smiled brightly. 'Right,' he said, clapping his hands together. 'Who fancies a nice big bag of crisps?'

With that, the entire potato army charged. Two hundred lumpy bodies thundered across the field, ignoring the Creeper's orders to stop.

'Ooh, they don't look happy,' Jake said.

'That's the idea!' Liam grinned. 'Go, sis!'

Sarah slammed her foot down on the accelerator. The back wheels spun, throwing mud into the air.

'Go, sis!' Liam said again.

The engine roared. The wheels spun. The potato-men closed in.

'Uh, slight problem,' said Sarah. She looked at the boys and smiled, weakly. 'It appears that we're stuck.'

CHAPTER FIFTEEN

LIAM'S EXPLOSIVE END

Jake and Liam jumped down from the tractor. The potato-men were just a dozen or so metres away and closing. Luckily, their misshapen bodies made it difficult for them to move quickly, but they would still be on them in just a few seconds. There was no time to lose.

'Push!' cried Jake, placing his hands flat on the back of the vehicle and shoving with all his might. Liam leaned his back against the tractor and dug his heels into the soft ground.

'I *am* pushing,' he groaned, his face turning a worrying shade of red from the effort.

The wheels spun on either side of them, spraying mud and dirt in their faces. They coughed and wheezed as they shoved and pushed and heaved and . . .

Yes! The tractor rumbled forwards, just as the nearest potato-person made a grab for Liam. He ducked, shrieking in panic, then scrambled back onto the tractor with Jake.

'Are they coming?' Sarah asked.

'They're right behind us,' Jake replied. 'Can't you make this thing go any faster?'

'It's lucky I can make it go at all,' said Sarah. She tapped a dial on the dashboard. 'We're almost out of fuel. We're running on fumes.'

Liam's face went pale. 'What? Why didn't you tell us that earlier?'

'I didn't notice,' Sarah admitted.

'You didn't notice?' Liam yelped. 'How could you not notice?'

'I was a little bit distracted by the evil supervillain and his army of killer vegetables!'

'Fair point,' Liam said. 'Well made.'

The tractor bounced through a ditch and slowed sharply, the engine shuddering. Jake, Liam, and Sarah all held their breath. If the tractor stopped now, there'd be no way of escaping the potato-people. They'd be done for.

'Please keep going, please keep going, please keep going,' Liam whispered.

Sarah dropped down a gear and pushed the accelerator pedal harder. The engine spluttered and coughed, then gave a roar. The tractor rumbled forwards, and Liam let out a sob of relief.

He cleared his throat, composing himself. 'Wasn't worried at all,' he said. 'Not for a minute.'

The tractor chugged across the uneven soil. The potato-men stumbled along behind. Liam watched them, then puffed out his cheeks. 'It's not a great chase scene, is it?' he said.

'What do you mean?' asked Jake.

'Well, if this was a movie, it wouldn't be a great chase scene,' said Liam, shrugging. 'We're only doing about two miles an hour.'

'If it was a movie, there'd be a dramatic soundtrack to make it more exciting,' Jake pointed out.

'Yeah, suppose,' said Liam. After a moment, he began to whistle a fast-paced tune. 'You're right,' he said, once he'd finished. 'That did make it seem more exciting.'

Up ahead, black smoke was billowing up from Professor Bloom's garden. They didn't need to look through the gap in the hedge to see the tree-throne now. It was several times larger than it had been when they'd left the garden, its branches and vines stretching out in all directions.

The closer they got to the garden, the more choking the smell of gas became. They all pulled the necks of their clothes up over their noses and mouths, trying to block out the stench.

'Jake, grab Max,' Liam said. 'Everyone get ready to jump.'

Jake scooped up the sleeping dog and held him tightly. 'Got him.'

'What if the spuds chase after us instead of the tractor?' Sarah fretted.

'They won't,' said Liam.

'How do you know?'

Liam smiled at his sister. It was a strange smile, she thought. Sad, almost.

'Because,' he said. 'They'll be chasing me.'

He slammed himself sideways, sending both Jake and Sarah sliding along the seat. They tumbled out of the tractor, just as Liam took the wheel.

'Ever tried potato fritters?' Liam bellowed over his shoulder. 'A bit like mash, but rolled in breadcrumbs and deep fried—delicious!'

Jake caught Sarah by the arm and pulled her away from the potato-people. Sure enough, the whole army was focused on catching the tractor—and Liam—and completely ignored Jake and Sarah as they raced past.

'Liam!' Sarah gasped, struggling against Jake's grip.

'He's going to get himself killed!'

'He won't!' Jake said. 'He knows what he's doing.'

'Come on, this is Liam we're talking about!' Sarah yelped.

Jake's face fell. 'You're right,' he realized. 'But it's too late. He's almost at the garden. There's nothing we can do for him now.'

Liam's teeth rattled as the tractor bounced and trundled across the uneven ground. The wheel seemed to be wrestling with him, fighting to steer him away from the rumbling, smoking garden that now lay just ahead.

Behind the tractor, two hundred potato-people were closing in. Each and every member of the army was there, their bulbous eyes bulging, their branch-like legs pounding across the soil.

The hedge was just a few seconds away now. Five. Four. Three.

Jake grabbed his spade and wedged the handle against the accelerator pedal. 'Here goes nothing,' he whispered, then he dropped from the tractor and rolled under the hedge. Tucked out of sight, he frantically commando-crawled towards the school, searching for somewhere to take cover.

The tractor rolled onwards through the gap in the hedge, making straight for Professor Bloom's machine. As the first of the potato-men followed it through, Liam powered along on his elbows, crawling frantically across the ground, trying to reach cover before—

KABOOM! The tractor smashed into the side of the shuddering machine. The now-mutated chair, the garden, and the ground below it, all erupted at once. The explosion hit the gas main, triggering a chain reaction of blasts which tore through the school, sending bricks, and glass, and bits of desk streaking through the air in every direction at once.

The blast swept across the horde of potato-men, roasting them and turning their skin a crispy shade of brown. Almost immediately, they began to explode like popcorn kernels in the microwave, their innards erupting up and outwards, becoming fountains of gooey white mash.

The back few rows of spud-creatures tried to turn and run, but they couldn't outrun the crackling flames or the chunks of rubble that came whizzing through the air towards them.

Far across the field, Jake and Sarah saw the fireball and felt the heat of it on their faces. They threw themselves to the ground and covered their heads with their arms as debris rained around them.

When the roar of the explosion had passed, and

the chunks of rubble had stopped falling, they slowly raised their heads.

The school was gone. There were bits of it left, yes—Jake could see part of the roof, and a tiny section of what looked like the maths corridor—but otherwise it was little more than a crater in the ground.

The garden was gone, too, along with Professor Bloom's throne-machine. In their place was an enormous quivering mound of gooey potato.

'Where's Liam?' Sarah asked, her eyes desperately scanning the carnage. 'Can you see him?'

Jake squinted, blinking against the cloud of dust and soil that hung in the air. He could see . . . something approaching them from the direction of the school. Was that him? Jake felt a surge of hope. Was that Liam?

A smouldering tractor tyre rolled past them, and Jake deflated. 'I can't see him,' he whispered. 'I can't see him anywhere.'

Sarah jumped to her feet and raced towards what was left of the school. 'Liam!' she cried. 'Liam, where are you?'

Jake hurried after her, still holding Max to his chest. 'Liam? Liam, mate, are you OK?' he called.

Somewhere in the distance, sirens blared. Someone had heard the explosion. No surprise, really. Jake's ears were still ringing from it, and he doubted there was anyone in town who wouldn't have felt the ground shake.

'He's not here!' Sarah said, tears springing to her eyes. 'I can't see him, Jake. He's not here!'

Inside the mound of mash, something moved. A lumpy, misshapen figure stumbled free, coated head to toe in slimy spud innards. One of the potato-

people had survived!

Sarah flew at it, fists flying. 'You killed my brother!' she screamed, thumping it hard. 'You monster! You killed my brother!'

She kicked the creature on the shin, then drove a fist against the side of its head.

'Ow!' it yelped, its voice muffled by the potato mush.

'Hurt, did it? How about this?' Sarah cried.

She slammed her shoulder into the monster's stomach and they both fell to the ground. Sarah punched and slapped at it, her face twisted in rage.

'Cut it out!' the monster protested. 'I'm telling Mum and Dad!'

Sarah stopped. She gasped. 'Liam?'

Liam scooped the potato from his face. 'Yeah, who did you think it was?'

'I thought you were a potato-monster!'

Liam snorted. 'Do I look like a potato-monster?' he said. He looked down at himself. 'Oh, wait. Yeah, I totally do.'

There was a big blob of fluffy spud on the end of his finger. He sniffed it.

'Don't,' said Sarah, clambering off him. 'Don't you dare!'

Liam touched his tongue against the stuff. Sarah and Jake both recoiled in horror.

161

'Not bad,' said Liam, then he popped the whole lot in his mouth and swallowed. 'Not bad at all.'

Liam got to his feet, immediately slid in the mashed potato, and fell over again. He stood up again, more carefully this time.

'So, it worked then,' he said, looking at the spot where the garden used to be. 'We blew up the army!'

'Yeah, that's not all we blew up,' said Jake, pointing to Liam's left.

Liam turned his head a fraction, then gave a little yelp of surprise when he saw the school. Or, more precisely, the lack of one. 'Ooh. Yeah. That's unfortunate,' he said. He shrugged. 'Sort of.'

He turned and grinned at his sister and friend. 'Oh well, all's well that ends well. It looks like we saved the day!'

'Not quite,' hissed the Creeper, gliding across the grass towards them. His face was twisted in rage, and his tentacle-like vines snapped at them like angry snakes.

'Oh yeah,' Liam muttered. 'Forgot about him.'

'You destroyed my army,' the Creeper snarled. 'My family.'

'Yeah,' said Jake, squaring up to the monster. 'We did.'

'And we'd do it again,' said Sarah, folding her arms.

'Especially if they're all this delicious,' added Liam, licking another dollop of potato off his hand.

The Creeper's eyes blazed an emerald green. 'Insolent fools! You think this is the end? You think you've stopped me? This is merely the beginning.'

His vines planted themselves in the ground and raised the Creeper into the air so he loomed high above Jake and the others. 'This is a minor setback. An inconvenience, at most.'

The sound of the sirens grew louder as several police cars and fire engines roared along the street approaching the school. 'I will return,' the Creeper said. 'I will take my revenge on all mankind!'

The vines retracted a little, bringing the monster closer. 'But mark my words, first I shall take my revenge on you three. It will be slow. It will be painful.' His lips curved into a thin smile. 'It will be *fun*.'

Liam gulped. 'Doesn't sound like fun,' he muttered.

'Oh it will be,' the Creeper promised. 'For me.'

He began to laugh. The ground beneath him parted. The Creeper kept his green-eyed gaze on Jake as he sank down into the soil, and was swallowed by the Earth.

Jake, Liam, and Sarah all stared at the ground in silence as the hole closed over. It was Liam who spoke first.

163

'Is it weird that I'm sort of going to miss him?' he asked.

'Yes,' said Sarah.

'Definitely,' agreed Jake.

'Weirdo,' Sarah added.

Max barked. Jake grinned. 'See, even the dog thinks you're strange,' he said.

Sarah kicked soil onto the spot where the Creeper had vanished. 'Do you think he meant that stuff he said?' she wondered. 'About coming back for us?'

'Probably,' said Jake. He shrugged. 'But it doesn't matter. We'll be ready for him. Besides,' he said, reaching into his pocket, 'we've got evidence now!'

He held up his mobile phone and smiled. The smile fell away almost at once, when he realized the phone had been smashed to bits at some point during the battle.

'Or maybe not,' he grimaced. He looked at his friends. He looked at the burning remains of the school. 'We're in so much trouble,' he said.

'Meh,' said Sarah, putting her arms around the boys' shoulders. 'We've been through worse.'

And with that, they turned away from the school, and walked in the direction of the approaching sirens.

CHAPTER SIXTEEN

HACKER'S FINAL THOUGHTS

So there we have it. That brings us to the end of this tale—or perhaps the beginning.

I was sent along to cover the explosion at the school for the Larkspur Chronicle. I jumped at the chance, of course. The last thing that had ever been blown up in Larkspur was the deputy mayor's dress, while she was opening the new town library on a blustery day. An explosion—an actual, real, proper explosion—was pretty much the most exciting thing I could think of.

Of course, that was before I learned about him. That was before I heard about the Creeper.

I overheard Jake, Liam, and Sarah telling the

police their story of this strange, plant-like man and his army of living potatoes. The police didn't believe them, of course. They got quite angry, in fact, and warned them they'd be in big trouble if they kept wasting police time.

Even when the kids pointed out that the school grounds were partly buried under several tonnes of lumpy mashed potato, the police said it probably came from the school canteen! I'm not sure how much mashed potato they think the pupils go through, but there was enough of the stuff lying around to feed ten schools. For a month.

Some people from the fire brigade moved the kids on then, but I hurried after them and asked them to tell me all about this Creeper character.

They seemed suspicious at first, but I managed to convince them they could trust me. What they told me—the things they said—shocked me to the core. It all sounded so utterly ridiculous, and yet they were so sincere that I couldn't help but believe them.

When the police weren't looking, I snuck into what was left of the school garden and had a good root around (no pun intended), hoping to find some sort of evidence. Aside from some chunks of wood, a few bits of scorched wiring, and more mashed potato than I've ever seen in my life, though, I found nothing that could prove the Creeper was ever there.

Jake's phone was too damaged to be any help, either. We managed to retrieve a single photograph, which Jake and the others insisted showed one of the potato-people. It was so blurry and smudged, though, that it could have been anything, really.

I told my editor about the story—the real story— but he was as sceptical as the police. He warned me that if I wrote that story, and didn't stick to what the police had said happened, then my career would be over.

And so, that's why the front page of The Larkspur Chronicle that week told the story of a leaking gas main beneath the school, and the terrible accident which had destroyed most of the building. That's the official story, even though it isn't what really happened.

Make no mistake, though—I will tell the true story of the Creeper sooner or later. I just need to gather some more evidence first, so I can expose him once and for all, and let the world see him for the monster he is.

I'm sure he'll strike again. After what he told Jake, Sarah, and Liam, I'm positive he'll come after them, seeking revenge. He blames them for destroying his army, but the irony is it was he himself who set the

167

machine to self-destruct. It was he himself who, along with Professor Bloom, had built the thing directly on top of the gas main.

I doubt he sees it that way, though. And, if I were Jake or his friends, I'd be sleeping with one eye open from now on, just in case the Creeper comes creeping back.

Oh, and by the way, Max was fine in the end. The vet checked him over, and it turned out he just had a lump on his head and a mild concussion. He's lucky that spud bullet wasn't half a centimetre lower, or he'd have been done for. He's up and about and as chirpy as ever now, although apparently he's slightly wary of vegetables, and no longer tries to steal the chips off Jake's plate at dinner.

Thanks for reading my Creeper Files. Until next time, this is Hacker Murphy, signing off. Stay safe out there, and remember—if your veg gets violent, or your saplings seem sinister, don't hang about. Run. Scream. Get away.

Because the Creeper might just be coming for you.

Your friend,
Hacker Murphy

ARE YOU BRAVE ENOUGH
TO HANDLE MORE

CREEPER FILES ?

READ ON FOR A TASTE OF

WELCOME
TO THE JUNGLE.

AVAILABLE NOW.

Jake Smith and his best mate, Liam, stepped back to admire their handiwork. Jake tilted his head left and right, trying to find an angle where the construction before them looked anything like it was supposed to.

'Ta-daa!' said Liam, grinning from ear to ear.

Liam's twin sister, Sarah, leaned past them and stared in wonder at what they'd built. 'What's that supposed to be?' she asked.

'It's a tent, obviously,' Liam said.

'It's inside out,' Sarah pointed out. 'The poles are supposed to be on the inside.'

Jake nodded. 'That's it. I knew there was something not quite right.'

Jake would be the first to admit that he was no

expert on tents, or the great outdoors in general, in fact. But when an opportunity to go on the school camping trip had come up, he and his friends hadn't been able to resist.

They'd recently come face-to-foliage with a monstrous creature they'd named the Creeper, and had barely survived to tell the tale. And tell the tale they had, only no one had believed a word of it. Not surprising, really, considering the tale involved exploding potato-men and a machine that turned people into plants.

After going through all that, a few days relaxing in the wilderness was well-deserved, Jake reckoned. If that meant escaping from having to take the dog out, empty the dishwasher, and do all his other chores back home, then so much the better!

It wasn't without its downsides, of course. Accompanying the group on the trip was Mr Campion, their exercise-obsessed head teacher. The good news was, he had arranged for them to do all kinds of fun activities, like abseiling, canyoning, kayaking, and more. The bad news was, he had woken them up at 6 a.m. that morning to go on a five mile hike through the forest, and planned to do so every day of the trip.

Liam had managed to sleepwalk through the hike, and only woke up when they arrived back at camp, just in time for breakfast. Mr Campion had tried to insist everyone eat only fruit and vegetables they foraged from the forest, but Sarah had pointed out that, as they weren't technically in school, his authority was limited, and—much to everyone's delight—had produced several packs of bacon from her rucksack.

Unlike Jake and Liam, Sarah was brilliant at camping. Then again, she was brilliant at most things, so that was no real surprise. She knew how to tie knots, navigate using the stars, and identify animal tracks.

She also knew what a tent was supposed to look like, and it was nothing like the teetering, inside-out jumble of plastic and canvas propped up on the grass in front of them.

'How many times is it you've tried building your tent now?'

'How many days have we been here again?' Liam asked.

'Less than one.'

Liam counted on his fingers. 'Nine times,' he said. 'But we've definitely got it this time.'

Right on cue, the tent collapsed.

'OK, almost got it,' Liam corrected.

Jake sighed. 'Maybe we should look at the instructions?'

'Hush your mouth!' Liam gasped, looking horrified.

'We're men, Jake. We don't need instructions! We can build things using instinct alone.'

A gust of wind caught the collapsed tent and swirled it up into a tree. Jake, Liam, and Sarah all stared at it in silence for a while.

'What are your instincts telling you now, then?' Sarah asked.

Liam puffed out his cheeks. 'They're telling me that we should've probably brought a ladder,' he said.

'Hmm. Interesting tent placement,' said a voice from behind them. The tone was annoyingly crisp and proper, with just a hint of amusement dripping from the ends. It was a voice they'd all grown pretty fed-up of over the past sixteen or so hours.

They turned to find Callum peering at them over the rim of his glasses, a lop-sided smirk on his face. None of them had exactly been Callum's number one fan in school, but out here in the wilderness he was proving to be even more annoying.

'I mean, it's unorthodox,' Callum continued. 'I don't imagine it'd be very comfortable, the way it's dangling from the branches like that, but each to their own, I suppose.'

'What do you want, Callum?' Jake asked.

'Oh, Jake,' said Callum, still smirking. He gestured over to his own tent. With its climate-adjusting air-conditioning and water-dispersing fabric, it looked like something that belonged on an Arctic expedition. 'What could you possibly give me that I don't already have?'

'A personality?' Sarah guessed.

'Friends?' asked Jake.

'Head lice?' said Liam.

'I don't have head lice!' Jake protested.

Liam shrugged. 'You will now you've shared a tent with me.'

'Aaaaanyway,' said Callum, cutting in. 'Delightful as this is, I came over here not because there's something you can do for me, but because there's something I can do for you.'

'Is it shut up and never talk to us again?' Liam asked. 'Because if it is, I'm very much in favour.'

Callum forced a smile. 'Hilarious,' he said, not laughing. 'No. I want to show you something I found.'

Jake sighed. 'Go on then, get it over with.'

'It's not here,' Callum said. 'It's in there.'

He pointed to an area of the woods where the tall trees had knotted together at the top, plunging the forest below it into near-darkness. Another breeze whistled through the leaves, making the branches around them creak ominously.

'What is it?' Jake asked.

'Come and see for yourself,' said Callum. He turned to walk away, then stopped and glanced back over his shoulder. 'Unless you're all too scared.'

Ten minutes of trudging through prickly bushes and overgrown undergrowth later, Jake, Liam, and Sarah found Callum waiting in a narrow clearing. The trees seemed more gnarled and twisted here, and Jake almost cried out in fright when a hand-like branch made a grab for his shoulder.

'It's just the wind,' Sarah whispered, seeing the shock on Jake's face. 'Just the wind and a normal branch. Nothing to worry about.'

Jake hoped she was right. After their last encounter, the Creeper had sworn he'd be back to take his revenge on them. Venturing out on a camping trip right beside an enormous forest filled with trees, plants, and other foliage, Jake was starting to realize, may not actually have been the best idea.

Still, there was no way he was going to let Callum see he was afraid, so he pushed away the branch, squared his shoulders, and tried his best to look tough.

Liam, on the other hand, was taking a very different approach.

'Eek! Bugs! Get them off!' he yelped, dancing in circles and frantically slapping at his face. A bluebottle was buzzing around him, easily dodging his flailing arms. Every time he tried to slap it, the insect flew away, circled Liam's head, then landed on his face again. As a result, Liam's cheeks were covered in red handprints, and the bluebottle was completely unharmed.

'It's a fly,' said Sarah. 'Calm down.'

'It's a giant killer space fly!' Liam said.

'It isn't,' said Sarah. 'It's just a normal fly. It can't hurt you.'

'Most people would say that about potatoes, too,' Liam pointed out, thwacking himself on the forehead. 'And look what happened there.'

'Wow,' said Callum. 'You three just talk and talk, don't you?'

He beckoned for them to follow him through a narrow gap in the trees ahead. Liam and Sarah fell into step behind Jake, picking their way carefully through the soggy tangle of grass and weeds.

'You don't think he's going to kill us, do you?' Liam whispered.

'Nah,' said Jake. 'Not all of us, anyway.'

'Probably just you,' Sarah added.

Liam swallowed. 'Haha. You're kidding,' he said. His eyes darted between them. 'You are kidding, right?'

Before either of them could answer, Jake stumbled out of the trees and into another clearing. All three of them gasped when they saw what stood ahead of them.

It was a tent. A tent which, by the looks of it, had been there for a very long time. Vines had crept across the canvas, almost completely covering it. The few patches of fabric they could still see were heavy with moss and mould.

The roots of the nearest few trees were tangled around the bottom, as if they were holding it down to stop it escaping. It looked as if it had been there for decades, and yet still somehow managed to look better than Jake and Liam's effort.

'What's this?' asked Jake.

'I think it's a tent,' said Liam.

'Well, I mean, obviously it's a tent,' said Jake. 'I meant why show us it?'

Callum shrugged. 'Oh, I dunno. Just thought you might find it cool. I stumbled upon it when I was exploring earlier. By my estimate, it's been here for at least forty years.'

A flicker of something wicked crossed his face,

unnoticed by Jake and the others. 'Dare you to open it and look inside,' he said.

'No way!' said Jake.

'Only an idiot would look in there,' scoffed Sarah.

'I'll do it!' chimed Liam, who never could resist a dare. He elbowed past his sister and best friend, then marched right up to the tent.

'Don't do it,' urged Sarah. 'There could be anything in there!'

Liam took hold of the zip. It was a little rusty, but still worked. 'You worry too much, sis,' Liam said. He pulled down, unfastening the door. 'What's the worst that could happen?' he asked.

And then he screamed as something reached out from within and dragged him inside.